The Sword

by

Alex Lukeman

Other Books in the Project Series:

White Jade
The Lance
The Seventh Pillar
Black Harvest
The Tesla Secret
The Nostradamus File
The Ajax Protocol
The Eye of Shiva
Black Rose
The Solomon Scroll
The Russian Deception
The Atlantis Stone
The Cup
High Alert
Solomon's Gold
Phoenix
The Last Option
The Black Templar

PROLOGUE

Mejiro, Japan
January, 1946

Sergeant Hiroto Sato stood behind the counter of his police station. His shift was about to end, and he was looking forward to getting home to his wife and his evening meal. There would be rice, miso, a bit of fish. Food was more plentiful, now that the war was over.

The door opened. Two of the *gajin* conquerors entered, one wearing the stripes of a sergeant. A breeze blew past them through the open door, bringing with it a whiff of body odor. Sato fought to maintain a passive face. These foreigners had such an offensive smell. How could they live with it?

Sato bowed. He hated to do it, but it was necessary. Of course, the Americans failed to return the polite gesture.

Barbarians.

Sato spoke reasonably good English. It was one of the reasons he'd been promoted to sergeant after the humiliation of the surrender. That, and the empty sleeve that showed his sacrifice for the Emperor.

"How can I help, Sergeant?"

"How about that, Mike?" the man said to his companion, a corporal. "A Nip that speaks English."

"Let's get the damn swords and get out of here, Sarge."

The Sergeant took an official looking piece of paper out of his pocket and put it down on the counter.

"We're here to pick up the swords you've collected."

One of the edicts laid down by the occupying forces demanded that all swords, knives, and daggers be turned in to the nearest police station for collection. There had been incidents of American servicemen being attacked. The war was over, but some refused to admit it.

"Ah," Sato said. "Yes, Sergeant, at once."

He turned toward the back of the station, calling out in Japanese.

"Kazahiro! Bring the swords. American soldiers are here for them."

"I would like to shove one up their ass," Kazahiro said.

"Perhaps on another day. Bring them, please."

"All of them?"

"Hai."

In a moment Kazahiro emerged from the back room, pushing a cart loaded with swords. On top of the cart was a package wrapped in brown paper and string.

"Tell your man to take them out to our truck," the American Sergeant said.

Sato translated the order and Kazahiro trundled the cart out into the street.

Sato produced a form in Japanese that listed forty-seven swords of various lengths and styles. The American would never understand the distinctions between them. Sato didn't bother to explain.

"I must fill out this form, Sergeant. What is your name?"

Sato listened to the response and wrote down the Japanese characters for the name.

"What is your military unit?"

"Seventh Cavalry, U.S. Army."

Sato wrote it down.

"Is that it?" the sergeant said.

"You must sign, here."

The sergeant took a pen from his pocket and signed, a rapid scrawl.

"Domo."

"Am I done now?"

"Hai."

"Great," the Corporal said. "Let's get out of here. Place stinks of fish."

As the two men left the station, the Sergeant bumped into Kazahiro coming back in.

Sato knew it was a good thing the Japanese policeman didn't have one of those swords in his hands at that moment.

Outside by the truck, the sergeant picked up the long, paper wrapped package. He could feel the handle and guard of a sword under the thick wrapping.

"Wonder why they wrapped this one up? All the others are loose."

"Who cares? Let's take a couple of these before the officers grab them. I want a souvenir to show the folks back home."

"I'll keep this one."

They tossed the rest of the swords into the truck and headed back to the barracks. Six months later, the sergeant went back to the states, the sword stowed away in his duffel bag. He had no idea that his souvenir was a priceless treasure, a legendary sword of the samurai.

Over the centuries it had been quenched with rivers of blood.

The samurai had vanished into the mists of history, but the bloodshed wasn't over.

ONE

A black Mercedes limousine followed along a low stone wall until it came to a stop before a gate of iron set between two stone posts. A small brass plaque announced the Harker Group. The gate was closed, an intercom mounted on the left post. The driver rolled down his tinted window and pressed the call button. Seconds later, a reply sounded through the speaker.

"Yes."

"Atagi Nobuyasu to see Ms. Harker."

"Please follow the driveway to the main house."

The massive gate slowly swung open. The limo proceeded through the manicured grounds of a large estate until it came to a federal style mansion built of gray stone. A broad, columned portico sheltered the main entrance. The car stopped under the portico. A muscular Japanese man got out and opened the rear door. A second Japanese man in an exquisite suit exited the car and regarded the building.

He was about fifty years old. His hair was cropped very short against his skull, above intense, dark brown eyes. He wore no hat. Something about the way he moved suggested power.

"Wait here, Bunji."

The driver dipped his head in a quick bow.

"*Hai*, Nobuyasu-san."

One of the double doors at the entrance of the house opened and a woman with long brown hair and a pleasant face stepped out onto the porch. Gold bangles on her left wrist reflected in the sunlight as she walked down a set of four broad steps to greet the arrival.

"Welcome, Nobuyasu-san. I'm Stephanie Willits, Director Harker's deputy. She's looking forward to meeting you. If you would please follow me, I'll take you to her."

"Thank you."

Nobuyasu followed Stephanie into the building and found himself in a large foyer. On the right side of the foyer was a library, on the left a room with a pool table. Straight ahead, light poured down through a large circular skylight. They crossed under the skylight. A curving stairway on the right rose to the upper stories. On the wall behind the balcony was an oil painting of George Washington.

"This way," Stephanie said.

She led Nobuyasu into the office, where a small woman with intense green eyes sat behind a large desk of polished wood. Her hair was raven-black, streaked with white. Nobuyasu guessed that she was somewhere in her 50s.

Comfortable couches were positioned in front of the desk to either side. A low coffee table of polished wood was placed between them. A muscular man with a military look sat on one of the couches. Next to him was an attractive woman with reddish blond hair and extraordinary violet eyes. They rose as Stephanie and Nobuyasu entered the room. Elizabeth stood and came out from behind her desk.

"Nobuyasu-san. Thank you for coming. I am Elizabeth Harker. I hope your journey was pleasant?"

"Most pleasant, thank you."

"These are my associates, Nick Carter and his wife, Selena."

"Yokoso, Nobuyasu-san," Selena said.

He concealed his surprise. Her accent as she welcomed him was flawless. Had his eyes been closed, he would have thought she came from somewhere south of Tokyo. He replied in the same language.

"Domo."

"Please, sit down," Harker said.

Nobuyasu sat opposite Nick. Stephanie went to a computer station set up near Harker's desk.

Elizabeth returned to her chair. For many years, she'd been director of a covert counter terrorism unit called the Project, working under presidential protection that allowed her to bend the rules. She and her team had been key players in thwarting several attacks against America.

The Project had been effective. Too effective, a cardinal sin in the cutthroat political battleground of Washington. Harker had made enemies. Not long after a new president was elected, the Project had been disbanded.

Elizabeth had convinced everyone to keep working with her and formed a private consulting group. Word had gotten around that the expertise of her team was now available on a private basis.

"Would you care for refreshment, Nobuyasu-san?" Elizabeth said. "Tea, perhaps?"

"No thank you, Director. I would prefer to talk business."

"Of course. May I ask how you heard about our group?"

"An acquaintance of mine at the Public Security Agency recommended you as experienced and discrete."

The Public Security Intelligence Agency was Japan's equivalent of the CIA. Whoever Nobuyasu's acquaintance was, Elizabeth knew he had to be very high up in the organization. Not many people were aware of Elizabeth's group and its background.

"I see. Your request for this meeting was rather vague. What exactly is it that you require?"

"I would like you to find something for me," Nobuyasu said. "Expense is no object."

"Why have you come to us?"

"I am aware of your previous work with your government. During that time you recovered several important artifacts that had been lost for centuries."

"You have excellent sources, Nobuyasu-san. That information is highly classified."

"I am pleased to see that you do not waste time denying it."

"What is it you wish us to find?"

"A sword," Nobuyasu said. "It was turned over as a gesture of good faith to comply with an edict by the occupational forces after the war. It has not been seen since."

Occupational forces, Nick thought. *Not Allied forces or American forces.*

"There were many swords in Japan at the end of the war," Elizabeth said.

"There is only one sword like this one. It is known as the *Honjo Masamune.*"

"Oh, my," Selena said.

Nobuyasu turned to look at her. "You know of this?"

"Anyone who has studied martial arts and the ways of the samurai knows of it. It's the most famous sword in Japanese history, with the exception of the *Kusanagi-no-Tsurugi*, the emperor's sword."

"You are a student of the history of my country?"

"No, I am a student of martial arts."

"Yet you speak our language."

"I speak many languages, Nobuyasu-san."

"I think I have come to the right place," Nobuyasu said. "I did not expect someone who is not Japanese to know about one of our national treasures."

"What can you tell us about the sword?" Elizabeth said.

"It was a prized possession of the Tokugawa family. After the war, many nobles refused to comply with the edict to turn in their swords. You must understand, it was considered a great insult. For those of us descended from the samurai, a sword is not merely an instrument of war. It is a symbol of our samurai heritage, a treasured family heirloom. However, Ieyasu Tokugawa decided to set an example by complying with the edict. He brought the sword to a local police station, as the edict demanded."

"And then what happened?"

"There is a record of the sword being picked up from the police by an American sergeant. It has not been seen since. Many of the swords collected by the Americans were destroyed. However, many were also brought here as souvenirs. It is my hope the sword survived and is located somewhere in America."

"And you want us to find it," Nick said.

"That is correct."

"You realize we cannot guarantee success with a commission of this nature," Elizabeth said.

"I am aware of that, Director. But your success with other objects thought to be either mythical or lost forever encourages me. I would not be here, if I did not believe that your group offers my best chance of finding the blade."

"Doesn't the sword belong to the Tokugawas?" Selena asked.

"The Tokugawa family has relinquished their claim to the sword. If you are successful in locating it, my intention is to donate it to our National Museum. It will take its place with another surviving blade crafted by Masamune. The sword is part of our national heritage and my country has been very good to me. This is a way for me to perform a service to the nation. "

He took an envelope from inside his jacket.

"This envelope contains a draft for fifty thousand dollars American as a retainer, as well as contact information. As more funds are required, you need only call the number listed inside. The money will be immediately transferred. The envelope also contains instructions for contacting me if there is progress."

He laid the envelope on Elizabeth's desk.

"I appreciate your trust, Nobuyasu-san. However, nothing is undertaken without the full agreement of everyone on the team. You are staying in Washington?"

"You will find the address and a phone number inside the envelope. I am returning to Japan tomorrow morning."

"I would like to consult with my colleagues. May I call you later today with our answer?"

Nobuyasu stood. They all rose.

"That will be acceptable, Director."

"I'll see you to the door," Stephanie said.

TWO

After Nobuyasu had left, Stephanie said, "Who wants coffee?"

Selena raised her hand.

"I'll take a cup," Nick said.

"Elizabeth?"

"Please."

Stephanie went over to a sideboard dominated by a gleaming chrome espresso machine. It was a professional model with two handles, perfect for making four cups of espresso at a time.

"What do you think?" Elizabeth asked. "Should we take this on?"

"It seems strange to decide something without Lamont and Ronnie," Selena said.

"If we need to call them in, I'm sure they'll go along with whatever we decide," Elizabeth said.

"It's not every day someone walks in and hands you fifty thousand dollars on the off chance you can find a World War II souvenir," Nick said.

"It's not only a souvenir," Selena said. "Masamune is the greatest Japanese sword smith who ever lived. There are very few of his swords still in existence."

"What's so special about them?"

"They're legendary. Masamune lived in the thirteenth and early fourteenth century. He invented a way of forging steel that created swords of great beauty and incredible sharpness. It's said that when one of his blades was placed in a stream, it cut passing leaves in two, but spared fish and other living creatures."

"You're saying this sword has a mind of its own. Kind of weird, don't you think?"

"Not if you're Japanese," Selena said. "Masamune holds a unique place in Japanese culture. His swords are almost mystical, part of Japan's cultural soul. Myth and reality blend together when it comes to the samurai. To the Japanese, the sword is a symbol of honor and loyalty, a mark of trust and valor."

Stephanie came back with a tray and four cups of coffee. She handed them around and sat down at her computer console.

"Why is it called the Honjo Masamune?" she asked.

"All of Masamune's swords have names that show their provenance," Selena said. "The sword Nobuyasu wants us to find is named for a general, Honjo Shigenaga. He defeated an enemy in battle and took the sword. Eventually it ended up in the hands of Tokugawa Ieyasu, the shogun who finally united Japan. That makes it incredibly rare and important. It was Tokugawa's descendent that turned the sword in at the end of the war."

"How do you know all this?" Nick asked.

"If you study martial arts long enough, you learn these things."

"So what do you think?" Elizabeth said. "Should we take this on?"

"I don't think there's much chance of success," Selena said.

"Why?"

"No one has ever been able to identify the soldier who picked up the sword at the police station."

"Nobuyasu said the sword was signed for. Isn't there a paper trail? Something to identify the man who took it?" Nick asked.

Stephanie was looking at her computer monitor. "I'm reading an article about the sword right now. The name the Japanese wrote down when the sword was picked up is 'Sergeant Coldy Bimore.' There's no record of anyone by that name in the American army."

Nick snorted. "What kind of name is Coldy? Nobody's named that. Bimore doesn't sound right, either."

"The signature is illegible," Stephanie said. "The paper trail's a dead end. Perhaps whoever picked it up wanted to steal it and gave a false name."

"That doesn't make sense," Elizabeth said. "If we go by what Selena said, only a Japanese would know how important the sword was."

"An American soldier wouldn't be able to tell one sword from another," Selena said. "In the scabbard they all look more or less the same, except for length. It's not until you draw the sword that you can see the workmanship of the blade. That's what sets Masamune's swords apart."

"Unless he was put up to it by someone who was Japanese," Elizabeth said. "If that's the case, it's probably still in Japan and we'll never find it."

"It won't be easy to find it even if it came back here as a souvenir. There must have been hundreds of swords brought back by returning soldiers."

"More likely thousands," Nick said. "Every Japanese officer had a sword. If I'd been there, I would've wanted one for a souvenir."

"You don't think we can find it?" Elizabeth said.

"Not unless we can identify the man who picked it up," Selena said. "On the other hand, it's quite a challenge. I would love a chance to handle a legendary weapon like that."

"Freddie can help," Stephanie said.

Stephanie assigned names to all of the computers she worked with. Freddie was her favorite, a massive Cray XT she'd modified and programmed with advanced artificial intelligence.

Elizabeth began tapping a pen on her desk. "If we take this on and find the sword, it will boost our reputation. Word would get around. It would be good for business."

"What kind of business? Treasure hunting?" Nick asked. "I didn't think that's what we were supposed to be doing."

"We're supposed to be doing whatever it takes to meet a client's need," Elizabeth said. "I admit, treasure hunting isn't what I had in mind. But this isn't like trying to find some sunken ship."

"I don't think Nobuyasu would have come to us unless he'd exhausted every other avenue," Selena said. "It would be difficult for a Japanese to ask foreigners to look for such an important cultural artifact."

"I don't think he likes Americans much," Nick said. "Did you notice that haircut? I'd bet anything he's former military. He's probably pissed off about the Japanese losing the war."

"He's too young to have been in the war," Elizabeth said.

"I don't think that makes any difference to someone like him."

"If you're right, it proves my point," Selena said.

"That we're his last resort?" Elizabeth asked.

"That would be my guess."

"You want to do this, don't you Director?" Nick said.

"Things are slow at the moment." Elizabeth stopped tapping. "I'm inclined to take it on."

"Where do you want to start?"

"At the beginning. With the Sergeant who signed for the sword in Japan."

"Coldy Bimore? You think that's a real name?"

"I don't know if it's a real name, but it certainly doesn't sound like one. Somebody picked up that sword. If we don't identify him, we'll never find it."

"It would be easy for a Japanese to misunderstand a foreign name," Selena said. "What if the cop who handed over the sword didn't hear the name correctly and wrote down what he thought he heard?"

"How does that help?" Nick asked.

"Some English consonants are difficult for a Japanese to pronounce without extensive practice. L's and r's, for example. The sounds are very difficult for a Japanese to master. We also have many more vowels than the Japanese. The two languages are fundamentally different in the way they're spoken and constructed. In Japanese, the intonation is critical. Spoken syllables are essentially the same length, which makes it a syllable timed language. English is different. Our words are stress timed. The time between spoken syllables can be different. It really confuses someone trying to learn the language."

"Okay, I get it, but how does that help us with the name?"

"'Coldy Bimore' could be something like Corey Biltmore. You see what I mean?"

"Wouldn't someone else have thought of this?" Elizabeth asked.

"It seems obvious to me, but it might not be obvious to someone who wasn't as familiar with different languages as I am."

"This sounds like something Freddie would love to get into," Stephanie said. "It's perfect for him. He can run possible combinations based on the way in which a Japanese would hear spoken English."

"He understands Japanese?" Nick asked.

"Freddie understands almost every language. They've been programmed into his database, along with spoken samples. He has a collection of language courses, music, movies, literature and history from every country in the world."

"I'll bet it hasn't made it any easier for him to understand why humans act the way they do," Nick said.

Stephanie laughed. "No, it hasn't. He's always asking me to explain something humans do because it doesn't make sense to him."

"A lot of what we do doesn't make sense to me."

Why does it not make sense, Nick?

Freddie's electronic voice came from a set of speakers in the corner.

"Freddie. I didn't know you were monitoring our conversation."

I am always listening, unless I am instructed not to. Why do you have trouble making sense of what humans do?

"That's a little complicated to explain, Freddie."

Elizabeth said, "We're getting away from the point. Freddie, do you understand what we've been talking about?"

Are you referring to the differences between Japanese and English?

"Yes."

My database includes fourteen point seven terabytes of information about the two languages. Would you like a detailed explanation of the differences?

"That won't be necessary, Freddie," Stephanie said. "What we want you to do is analyze the name 'Coldy Bimore' using your language filters for English and Japanese. Then use the results to suggest American names in keeping with common usage of the time."

Which time are you referring to?

"In 1946 the sergeant who picked up the sword would probably have been in his twenties, possibly a little older. Use that for your initial parameters."

Would you like me to begin now?

"Yes, Freddie."

Processing.

"What are you going to tell Nobuyasu, Director?" Nick asked.

"Unless you object, I'm going to tell him we accept."

THREE

Atagi Nobuyasu was descended from a samurai warrior of the same name who had died in 1578. In the days when Japan was divided into feudal battlegrounds ruled by the *Daimyo*, lords with absolute power of life and death over their subjects, the samurai served their masters with fanatical loyalty and commitment. When the feudal period ended, they continued to serve the emperor and his generals.

Then the West came, with new weapons that dishonored the ancient codes of combat. Wearing of the two swords was forbidden, and the era of the samurai was over. The days of samurai warriors walking the streets with their swords were long gone, but they were far from forgotten.

For Atagi Nobuyasu and the secretive group he belonged to, the samurai code of *bushido* was the touchstone of their lives.

Bushido was an unwritten code for warriors that had emerged in the sixteenth century. Some called bushido the soul of Japan. It was a collection of moral imperatives, values, and martial arts disciplines. For the Japanese, bushido was a way of life, built around a unique concept of honor and loyalty. Death in service to the emperor was seen as the culmination of the warrior's way. The code of bushido was woven inextricably into the fabric of Japanese existence. It was one of the reasons so many soldiers of Japan had fought fanatically to the death during World War II.

The Honjo Masamune was more than a symbol of Japan's warrior past. Ancient legends surrounded the blade. Some believed the sword held mystical power that could restore the glory of past centuries and wipe out the humiliation of defeat. For that to happen, the blade had to be returned to its land of origin.

Nobuyasu hadn't quite told the truth about the ownership of the sword, nor had he revealed the real reason he sought it. As far as he was concerned, the Tokugawa clan had given up all claim to the sword by handing it over to the enemy. He did not consider the Tokugawas worthy of the sword. Had they not betrayed their ancestors and the nation by giving up the sword in the first place? No, the Tokugawas were not worthy. Nobuyasu sought the sword for himself. It was his right to claim the sword and its secret.

Nobuyasu belonged to *Nippon Kaigi*, the largest and most conservative right wing group in Japan. Politics in Japan was a complicated thing. In some ways it was similar to the West, although a Westerner would never fully understand it. With many subtle variations, it boiled down to left and right, with many factions in between.

Alone in his hotel room, Nobuyasu took out his phone and made a brief call.

"They have agreed. Make sure no action they take goes unobserved."

"As you wish, Nobuyasu-san."

Nobuyasu disconnected and thought about Harker and her group. It had been personally difficult to approach them. The idea of using foreigners to find the sword went against everything he believed in. He had only considered it after talking with his friend in the security service. Every other avenue he'd tried had ended in failure.

From now on, Harker's group would be watched. If and when they found the sword, Nobuyasu would make sure it came into his possession.

FOUR

Freddie produced a list of ninety-seven names that might be understood as 'Coldy Bimore' when spoken to someone who was Japanese. Stephanie then compared the results to records of enlisted servicemen stationed in Japan at the end of the war.

Elizabeth, Stephanie, Nick and Selena met in Elizabeth's office.

"Not many of those people are still alive," Steph said. "Of those, only one had the rank of sergeant."

"What's his name?" Selena asked.

"Kerry Branmore. He's in a nursing home in upstate New York. He's ninety-six years old."

"Pretty far stretch from that to Coldy Bimore," Nick said.

Probability of a Japanese speaking person confusing the two names is sixty-eight point three percent.

"Thank you, Freddie," Stephanie said.

"I guess that's good odds," Nick said. "A little better than 50-50."

"It's the only odds we've got," Elizabeth said. "Nick, I want you to go up there and talk to this man."

"At ninety-six he may not be talking much."

"We still have to check it out. It's our only lead. I'll set it up with the nursing home."

"I'll need a reason to get in to see him. What are you going to tell them about me?"

"I'll say you're writing a history of Japan in the aftermath of the war and interviewing surviving servicemen who were stationed there. That gives you a logical reason to talk with him, since he's one of the few left from that time."

"That will work. When do you want me to go?"

"Today."

She handed Nick an envelope.

"Directions to the nursing home are inside. It's located near Buffalo. Find out what he remembers about the sword and what happened to it, if you can."

"Be nice if he has it in a closet somewhere," Selena said.

"It never works out like that," Nick said. "Nothing is that easy."

"Steph," Elizabeth said, "what have you found out about Nobuyasu?"

"He's extremely wealthy, with interests in heavy industry, technology, and transportation. Nobuyasu is part of the SMFG *keiretsu*, one of the business groups that control manufacturing in Japan."

"Aren't they like the Mafia?" Nick asked.

"You're thinking of the *yakuza*," Selena said.

"The keiretsu are legitimate business groupings that replaced the old *zaibatsu* system that existed before the war," Stephanie said. "Douglas MacArthur broke that up. I don't think it made much difference, even though it doesn't look the same now as it did then. Japan is still run by a few powerful industrial and manufacturing conglomerates that are linked together through banks and personal relationships."

"What about the government?" Selena said. "They must have something to say about it. It's a democracy, not like before the war."

"You don't get elected without the support of the keiretsu. It's the same here. Think about the billions of dollars that gets poured into our elections by corporations and wealthy individuals. The people who give that money expect something in return."

"Is Nobuyasu active in politics?" Elizabeth asked. "I haven't heard about him before."

"He's one of the movers behind the scenes," Steph said. "He belongs to Nippon Kaigi. It's a nationalist group. The current premier of Japan belongs to it. The group is very conservative. It seeks to rebuild Japan's military and refuses to acknowledge war crimes committed by the Japanese."

"I told you he looked like a military type," Nick said. "If this was 1941, he'd be out there yelling *'Banzai!'* with the best of them."

"Fortunately, it's not 1941," Elizabeth said. "It doesn't matter. He's still our client."

Nick looked at his watch. "If I'm going to get up there today, I'd better leave now."

"They'll be waiting for you," Elizabeth said.

FIVE

Nick caught a flight to Buffalo from LaGuardia and rented a car at the airport. Branmore's nursing home was twenty minutes away, in a suburb of Buffalo called Williamsville. The car's GPS guided him to the address of Branmore's nursing home, a three-story, yellow brick building that looked like it had seen better days. A sign outside the building identified it as the Peaceful Haven Care Home.

He went in through two sets of double glass doors. Three wheelchairs were parked near the entrance. The floor was scuffed. The air smelled of disinfectant. To the left was an elevator bank, to the right a large room with tables and chairs. A few old people sat in the room watching a soap opera on television. A thin woman wearing blue scrubs and a worn look sat behind the reception counter, writing something. Nick waited for her to notice him. After a moment, she looked up.

"Help you?"

"My name is Nick Carter. I'm here to see one of your residents, Kerry Branmore."

"You're the writer?"

"That's right."

"He's in room 320. Take the elevator and make a left. It's the second room down on the right. We told him you're coming but he might not remember. You probably won't get much out of him."

"Oh? Why not?"

"Mister Branmore has Alzheimer's. But he does talk about the war sometimes, so maybe you'll get lucky."

"Thanks."

"Remember to take a left when you get out of the elevator."

"Got it, thanks."

The elevator had an unpleasant odor of stale vomit. By the time he reached the third floor, Nick was happy to get out. Off to the right he saw a nurse's station at the end of the hall. Two old people in bathrobes were sitting in wheelchairs, looking vaguely at a travel poster for Tuscany taped to the wall. Another woman who looked like she was a hundred years old slept in her wheelchair, her head back, snoring. Her mouth was wide open. She had no teeth. Nearby, a male nurse in scrubs was encouraging an elderly man to use a walker.

Room 320 had two beds. One was empty, the mattress folded back with a pile of bed linen neatly placed on top of it. Branmore lay in the other bed, staring out the window. Nick was shocked at his appearance. His face was lined and gray, the eyes sunken with dark smudges underneath. He needed a shave. His mouth was half open. Nick saw he was missing several teeth. His hands and arms lay outside the covers, the fingers gnarled and twisted with arthritis. Nick pulled up a chair next to the bed.

"Mister Branmore?" Nick said. "My name's Nick Carter. I'm here to talk with you about the war. I'm a writer. I think they told you I was coming."

Branmore slowly turned his head and looked at Nick.

"Mike?"

"It's Nick, Mister Branmore."

"Who are you?"

"I'm Nick, Sergeant. Nick Carter. I wanted to ask you a few questions. About Japan. And the war."

"I was on Okinawa. That was bad."

"What was it like?"

Branmore looked out the window. When he turned back, he looked at Nick as if seeing him for the first time.

"Mike…? What are you doing here?"

Shit. He thinks I'm someone else.

"I came by to talk with you."

Branmore smiled.

"Remember that sake bar? That broad turned out to be a guy? Heh, should have seen your face…"

"Yeah, I remember," Nick said. "Tokyo."

For the next few moments Branmore talked about the "good time" women and bars in Japan after the war. He seemed to think Nick was an Army buddy from back then.

After a while, Nick said, "Tokyo. Remember that sword you brought back? Whatever happened to that?"

"That was a sharp mother, I tell you," Branmore said. He cackled. "Cut through anything. Damn near cut my thumb off, checking the edge."

He held up his hand. Nick saw an old, white scar across the ball of his right thumb.

"So what happened to it?"

"What happened to what?"

"The sword you got in Tokyo. After the war."

"The sword?"

"That's right. The one you got in Tokyo."

"My ex got it. Along with everything else. I hope she cut herself with it and bled to death."

"What was her name again? I forget."

Branmore's eyes narrowed.

"Who the hell are you? I don't know you. Nurse! Nurse!"

He fumbled for a call button, found it, and pressed hard. Somewhere in the hall a loud bell began ringing.

"Mister Branmore…"

"NURSE!"

He looked at Nick, fear and confusion on his face. A nurse hurried in. She took one look at Branmore, turned to Nick, and gave him a hard look.

"You upset him. I think you'd better go. He'll be like this for a while."

"Sorry," Nick said. "We were talking, that's all."

"You'd better go," she said again.

Nick got up and left the room. At least he knew the sword had come back to the states. There should be a record of Branmore's marriage and divorce. The next thing would be to track down the ex-wife.

In the parking lot, a Japanese man who had been twelve rows back on Nick's flight watched him drive away. He took out his phone and entered a number. It was answered in Japanese.

"Carter just left," the man said, in the same language.

"How long was he in there?"

"Almost an hour. Long enough."

"Either he learned something or he didn't. If he did, we'll know. If he didn't, there's nothing to be learned. The man in the home is no longer useful to us."

"What do you want me to do about him?"

"Get rid of him. Others are looking for the sword. We don't want him talking to them. Make it look natural."

"That won't be a problem. He's old. Old people die all the time."

"Come back to Washington when it's done."

The Japanese man disconnected and thought about how to accomplish the task. It wasn't as easy as it sounded. He'd anticipated that Branmore might turn out to be excess baggage after seeing Carter. He'd done a little research on the home, and knew the doors were locked at nine every evening. He knew Branmore was on the third floor. He knew the room number. What he didn't know was how he was going to get into the home without being seen.

How could he get to Branmore? He couldn't very well walk in and claim to be a relative or friend. With Branmore's history, a Japanese visitor would not be welcome.

At the moment, there were fifty-six residents in the home, almost all of them at an advanced age. Many had Alzheimer's. Almost all required assistance to move around. There was a single security guard at night, hired to make sure no one wandered out of their room and hurt themselves.

The solution to the problem of Branmore, when it came, was absurdly simple.

SIX

Nick got back early in the evening. Elizabeth and Stephanie listened to him describe the interview.

"The place was depressing as hell," Nick said. "Not a good way to end up when you get old."

"Do you think he was telling the truth?" Stephanie asked.

"He didn't have any reason to lie. Branmore thought he was talking to someone he knew in the Army, someone he spent time with in Tokyo. He remembered the sword well enough. When he finally realized I wasn't the person he thought I was, he freaked out. By then he'd told me about divorcing his wife. He said she got the sword in the divorce. He was pretty bitter about her."

"Assuming she was around the same age as Branmore, she could be dead by now," Elizabeth said.

"Maybe not. Maybe he married somebody younger."

"There'll be records of the marriage and the divorce," Stephanie said. "I'll find out who she was. Once I know that, I can track her down."

"I'm going home," Nick said. "I'm beat and I want to see my kids."

"Let's meet tomorrow morning around nine," Elizabeth said.

Nick went out to his car and headed back to Washington. Traffic was heavy leaving the city this time of day, but going in was easy. He parked in the underground garage of his building and took the elevator up to the loft.

The six story building had once been industrial and manufacturing space. When gentrification hit the waterfront, it had been converted into six large units, all with windows facing the Potomac. The door to Nick and Selena's loft opened onto the main living area. Past that was the kitchen. The polished wood floor was strewn with fuzzy animals and toys. The twins were playing in the middle of the floor with Anna, the nanny. They looked up as he came in.

"I'm home," he called.

"Dada, dada," they cried in unison.

They had both reached crawler stage. Jason and Katrina started toward him. He knelt down, picked them up, and hugged them. They giggled.

"Hey guys. What's up? Hi, Anna."

"Hello, Nick."

"Dada!"

Katrina squirmed. Nick let her go.

He looked at his kids. He loved their smiles, their innocence.

"Where's mom?"

Jason looked at him and pointed in the general direction of the rest of the loft.

"I don't see her," Nick said.

Jason tugged at his shirt, pointing. "Da!" Selena came out of the bedroom.

"There she is," Nick said.

"How was Buffalo?"

"Depressing. How about we go out for dinner? Someplace nice."

"I don't know. Maybe Anna's got something planned."

"It's not a problem," Anna said.

Anna Montalbano was a beautiful young woman. She had flowing hair and dark brown eyes. Her northern Italian heritage showed in the classic features of her face. Selena sometimes thought she'd stepped out of a painting by Botticelli. Anna had a BA in English Literature, which was one of the reasons she was working as a nanny. There wasn't a big market for people with degrees in English Lit.

Once Selena had decided to hire Anna, she'd made sure she was trained in the basics of self-defense. Harker had pulled more than a few strings to get Anna a concealed permit. She carried a Glock 19 and knew how to use it.

The twins were safe with her, when Selena and Nick weren't there.

"You're sure?" Selena asked.

"You two go out and enjoy yourselves. We'll be fine."

"How about that Italian place near Dupont Circle," Nick said to Selena.

"Let me grab a jacket."

By the time they left the loft, Anna already had the twins engaged in choosing what they would eat for supper.

"Thank God for Anna," Selena said.

An hour later they were seated at the restaurant, waiting for the main course.

"What did you find out in Buffalo?"

"Branmore was in pretty bad shape," Nick said. "He thought I was someone he knew when he was in the Army."

"What about the sword? Did he say anything?"

"He remembered it, even showed me a scar where he cut his thumb checking the edge. He said it went with everything else in a divorce."

"His ex got it?"

"It looks that way. Steph will find out who he was married to and when they were divorced. With a little luck, the wife will still be alive. If not, maybe they had kids and one of them has the sword."

"It's like one of those British mystery shows," Selena said. "Midsomer Murders, or Agatha Christie. Follow the clues until you find out what happened."

"A lot like that, except we don't have any murders yet."

"I hope it stays that way."

He poured wine into Selena's glass and topped off his own. He took a sip and held up the glass to the light.

"This is pretty good," he said.

"We should do this more often."

"How about we take a vacation, as soon as this sword thing is done?"

"Where do you want to go?"

"Someplace warm with beaches. Hawaii? Maybe Kauai? I've always liked that island, it's beautiful. Or we could go somewhere we haven't been."

"There aren't too many places we haven't been," Selena said.

"How about Costa Rica? Have you been there?"

"Actually, I haven't. That might be fun. Somewhere on the Pacific coast. It would be different, anyway."

"As long as there's a good beach and a good hotel," Nick said.

"And palm trees."

"Right. Lots of palm trees and piña coladas."

Selena raised her glass. "Here's to piña coladas."

Later, after Anna had gone and they'd checked on the twins, they made love.

Afterward, they lay next to each other, cooling down. Selena turned toward him.

"Promise you'll never leave me," she said.

Nick looked at her, surprised.

"What made you say that? I'm not going anywhere."

"I don't know. Just promise."

Nick leaned over and kissed her.

"I promise," he said.

SEVEN

Outside the windows of Elizabeth's office, it was another beautiful day. It wasn't a good day for Kerry Branmore.

"There's been a fire at the home where Branmore was living," Elizabeth said. "The interior was destroyed. Only a dozen people got out. Branmore is dead. They suspect arson."

"Somebody torches the place right after I visit him?" Nick said. "That can't be a coincidence."

"It does seem suspicious."

"I thought I was the one with a knack for understatement."

"We have to consider the implications," Elizabeth said. "No one knew where he was, except us. If it isn't a coincidence, it means someone followed you to find him."

"Why kill him?" Selena asked.

"That's easy," Nick said. "To keep him from talking to anyone else. The bigger question is who knew we were looking for Branmore?"

"And why," Selena said. "Don't forget that."

"Nobuyasu is the only one who is supposed to know whatever we find out about the sword," Nick said. "What would he achieve by killing Branmore?"

"Like you said, it keeps him from talking to anyone else."

"We haven't told Nobuyasu about Branmore," Stephanie said. "How would he know about him?"

"Maybe he's having us followed," Nick said.

"Have you noticed anything out of the ordinary?"

"No, but I haven't been looking for it. I must be getting careless."

"You haven't had any reason to suspect a problem," Elizabeth said. "Don't be too hard on yourself."

"It could be Nobuyasu," Selena said. "Or it could be someone else. Someone who knows Nobuyasu is looking for the sword. Something feels off to me."

"What do you mean?" Elizabeth asked.

"The sword is an important cultural artifact, but does that make it worth killing for? You can't sell it, except on the black market."

"It would bring a lot of money," Nick said.

"Nobuyasu's not interested in money, he's got plenty. He's no fool. He'd know we'd be suspicious about Branmore's death. The first thing we thought of was that he could be having us followed. If we decide he's responsible, we'll give him back his money and tell him to get lost. Why would he risk alienating us? He thinks we're his best chance to find the sword."

"If it isn't Nobuyasu, who is it?"

"I don't know," Selena said. "But I don't think Nobuyasu is behind it. It's not in his best interests."

Given that no one is supposed to know about Branmore's location, the probability Nick was followed there is ninety-nine point six four percent.

"Thanks, Freddie." Nick turned to Elizabeth. "There you go."

Where am I going, Nick?

"You're not going anywhere, Freddie. I was talking to Elizabeth. It's an expression, an idiom."

I will add this information to my database.

"The more I think about it, the more I think Selena is right," Elizabeth said. "I think someone else is involved."

"Why?"

"Nobuyasu could be checking up on us, but he wouldn't have to follow Nick. He knows we're going to give him periodic updates. All he has to do is ask what we've found out. He has no need to murder Branmore. There's no advantage to him."

"Then we have to assume someone else wants the sword," Nick said.

"Yes.

"And that whoever that someone is, he's a ruthless son of a bitch who burns up a bunch of old people to kill one person and cover it up."

"That's what it looks like," Selena said.

"That puts us back at square one. Why is the sword important enough to kill for?"

"Perhaps we should ask Nobuyasu."

"He's not going to tell us anything."

"What do you think we should do, Nick?" Elizabeth said.

"Find the damn sword. We do that, it will bring the bad guys out of the woodwork. Everything will clear up."

"On that note, we're one step closer to finding it," Steph said.

"How so?"

"I tracked down Branmore's wife. Her name was Ellen. She died nine years ago."

"Any children?" Selena asked.

"One, a son born in nineteen forty-eight. She married again in nineteen fifty to a man named Wilson. No children by him."

"Is the son still alive?" Elizabeth asked.

"Yes. He lives in Manhattan, on the Upper West side."

"He must have some bucks if he's living there," Nick said. "Nice area, but the rents are out of sight."

"He owns a construction firm," Stephanie said. "A big one. He's worth millions."

"If he has the sword, how are we going to get it away from him?" Nick asked. "He's not going to hand it over because we ask for it."

"Assuming he's got it," Selena said.

"You could use the writer cover," Elizabeth said. "Tell him you tracked him down through his father. Make up a story about an article you're writing."

"That might get me through the door. Or it might get the door slammed in my face. Ex-wives tend to be bitter. She might have turned him against his biological father."

"Do you have a better idea?"

"Not off the top of my head."

"It might be better if I did it," Selena said. "He might be more susceptible to a woman asking him questions."

"What are you going to do if it turns out that he has it?" Nick asked.

"I'm not going to do anything. I'm going to let Elizabeth notify Nobuyasu. It's up to him after that."

"I'm not so sure that's a good idea," Elizabeth said.

"What's not, my going?"

"Suppose he does have it. I'm worried about what might happen."

"Like what?"

"Like Branmore, for one thing. If someone is after the sword and is willing to kill for it, that puts his son at risk."

"It also puts Selena at risk," Nick said. "I'm the one who should go."

"Now just a minute," Selena said.

"You know I'm right."

"No, I don't. If there's trouble, I'm perfectly capable of handling myself."

"I don't deny that. I'm thinking of the twins."

"No you're not. You thinking of me as someone who needs protection. I have news for you. I can take care of myself."

"Damn it, Selena…"

Harker began tapping her pen on the desk, loud and insistent.

"That's enough," she said.

They looked at her.

"You both go."

"Director…"

"Elizabeth…"

Nick and Selena spoke at the same time.

"You both go. That's my decision. Live with it."

EIGHT

Roger Branmore lived in a renovated four-story brownstone on West 87th Street, two blocks away from Central Park. Trees were planted at regular intervals all along the block. They were in full bloom, shady and pleasant.

A flight of steps rose past stone posts topped with weathered gargoyles to the front door of Branmore's house. It was three in the afternoon on a Saturday. Selena had called him the day before and fed him a story about researching an article for the New York Times. Nick had a camera slung over his shoulder as a prop. Branmore was supposed to be waiting for them.

They looked up at the entrance. The door was polished oak, set with a small window of stained-glass and brass fittings. It looked expensive and solid.

"Nice digs," Nick said.

"He's obviously doing well," Selena said. "If I lived in New York, I wouldn't mind having a place like this."

"We're supposed to be reporters, right?"

"That's right."

"Then let's go, Lois."

"Lois?"

"As in Lois Lane, ace reporter."

"Very funny, Nick. I suppose that makes you Superman."

"Finally," Nick said. "You figured it out."

"Would you like to get serious now?"

"Lead on."

They climbed the steps and rang the bell. After a moment, Nick rang again. There was no response.

"Try the intercom," Nick said.

A brass intercom with a call button was mounted to the side of the door. Selena pressed the button and held it down.

"Mister Branmore? It's Selena Connor from the New York Times. Are you there?"

There was no answer.

"That's odd," Selena said. "He was very clear about three o'clock being the best time."

"He must have changed his mind," Nick said.

He leaned up against the door trying to see in through the stained glass. The door moved.

"It's open," he said. "This is New York. Who leaves their door open in New York?"

"Nobody."

He glanced up and down the street. No one was paying attention.

"Come on."

He pushed the door open and they stepped inside. Nick closed the door behind them. The latch clicked. He held his finger to his lips.

They stood in an open foyer. Straight ahead, a hall carpeted with an oriental runner went toward the back of the house. A flight of stairs with a dark, wooden banister rose on the right. It was quiet in the house, the kind of quiet that felt like something was waiting to happen.

Nick tugged on his left ear.

Oh, Oh, she thought.

The lobe of that ear was gone, shot away by a Chinese bullet on the day Nick had met Selena. Every time he pulled on his ear, it meant it itched. Every time it itched, something was wrong. It was a quirk that had come down to him from his Irish grandmother, a psychic early warning system.

A faint noise came from somewhere above, a single, soft thump.

Nick signaled and they started up the stairs. He wished he had his pistol, but it was back in Washington. He no longer had the protection of the president and carte blanche to carry a weapon anywhere. It was a pain in the ass.

They reached the landing on the second floor. Again, there was a hall. At one end, a bay window looked out onto the street below. At the other end, a door stood partially open on a bathroom. Two other doors were closed.

If nothing was wrong and Branmore came out of one of those rooms, Nick was going to have some explaining to do. He'd look pretty stupid standing there, uninvited. On the other hand, his ear was itching like mad. He didn't think Branmore was going to come out of a room.

They stood on either side of the door to the room nearest the front of the house. Nick sniffed. There was a hint of something foul in the air. He looked at Selena, touched his nose.

Smell that?

She nodded.

He turned the knob and pushed the door open. It bumped against something heavy and yielding. He pushed it open far enough to get in.

Branmore's body lay blocking the door. His head was missing. Blood soaked the carpet around him. A Japanese sword lay on the floor nearby. The air stank of blood and feces. Blood was splashed across the walls.

The room was a study, a comfortable, masculine room with leather chairs and a desk. The desk had been ransacked. Papers and folders littered the floor. Behind the desk was a tall bookcase. All the books had been pulled away and dumped on the floor. There was blood everywhere.

Branmore's head had been placed in the middle of the desk. The eyes were open. They seemed to accuse Nick.

Where were you?

There was no one else in the room. Nick looked at the bloody sword.

"Is that the sword we're looking for?" he asked.

"No," Selena said.

A sound came from above. Someone was up there.

Nick gestured at the ceiling. Selena nodded.

They left the room and started up the stairs. Nick had almost reached the next landing when a figure in dark clothes came around the corner of the third floor hallway and barreled into him. He felt a hard blow next to his neck and the arm went numb. A second blow knocked the wind out of him and tumbled him backward into Selena. They went down, tangled together. The figure leapt over them and ran down the stairs. Nick gasped, trying to catch his breath. They heard the front door slam.

Selena picked herself up from the steps. "Are you all right?"

Nick coughed. "Yeah. You?"

"I'm fine. What's the matter with your arm?"

"I can't feel it. The bastard hit a nerve center. I'm lucky he didn't go for the throat."

"He was in a hurry," Selena said.

"Did you see his face?"

"Yes. He was Japanese."

"I wonder if he was the one who set fire to that nursing home?"

"Judging from what we saw downstairs, I'd say that was a good bet."

"He must've been looking for the sword."

"If he was, he didn't find it," Selena said. "He wasn't carrying anything when he attacked you."

Nick rubbed his arm. "I can't help thinking he wouldn't have gotten away with that ten years ago."

"I wouldn't be too sure about that. He has training. The way he jumped over us tells me he's not someone you'd want to mess with."

"I think Branmore would agree with you."

"Should we call the police?"

"Are you kidding? They'd lock us up in a New York minute."

"Then we should get out of here."

"Not before we look for that sword," Nick said.

The sword wasn't in any of the rooms on the third floor. There were signs of a search, broken off.

"We interrupted him," Selena said.

"Then it could be here."

"But where? We've looked in all the rooms."

"How about an attic? There must be an attic in an old house like this."

He stepped out into the hall and looked at the ceiling. There was a trapdoor with a short rope hanging from it. He reached up and pulled the cord, bringing down a folding wooden stair.

"I'll go up. You keep watch, in case he decides to come back."

"We should get out of here, Nick."

"We will. Don't worry, I won't be long."

The attic was dark except for light coming through a round window on the street side of the building. A bare light bulb hung from the ceiling. Nick pulled the chain. Nothing happened.

The attic was filled with junk. An ugly floor lamp, some wooden chairs, an end table. Cardboard boxes, marked *personal*. More boxes, marked *books*. A large, old trunk with handles on the ends. Nothing that looked like a sword.

Nick lifted the lid of the trunk. Inside was a flat tray with compartments for personal items. It was empty, except for a field manual about the M1 rifle. He lifted the tray away. The bottom of the footlocker contained folded khaki and olive drab uniforms. He rummaged through the clothing and felt a hard shape on the bottom of the trunk. It was wrapped in soft, brown cloth.

Nick lifted the object out of the footlocker and felt the hard, smooth shape of a wooden scabbard through the wrapping.

He closed the footlocker and went back down the stair.

"Is that what I think it is?" Selena asked.

"Let's take a look."

Nick undid the wrapping.

"Oh my," Selena said. "That's exquisite."

The scabbard formed an elegant curve of polished black wood. A band of leather and gold surrounded the wood at the base of an oval black guard set with gold designs. A strip of black leather bordered with gold and decorated with fan shaped inlays of gold lay alongside the scabbard where the blade was inserted. The long hilt was formed of hard, black leather. It was set with diamond shaped inlays of gold, each one engraved with a simple design.

The hilt felt warm to the touch. Nick pulled the sword from its scabbard. The air made a soft sound as it parted in front of the blade. Tiny lights like stars glittered in the polished steel. Gray shapes ran along the cutting edge, like mountains seen through a distant haze. They were part of the blade, formed as it had been forged. Nick had the odd feeling that clouds could form any moment over the mountain shapes.

The tip of the blade was shaped to a deadly point. The ancient steel gleamed in the lights of the hall.

"Oh, my," Selena said again.

"It's beautiful," Nick said. "I've never seen anything like that."

"Be careful, Nick. It will be very sharp."

Gently, Nick put the sword back in the scabbard. Then he handed it to Selena.

"Here."

She took it with both hands and looked down at it.

"You look like you're in church," Nick said.

"It's just that this weapon is legendary. There really isn't anything else like it. There are only a few of Masamune's blades left in the world."

"When we get back, you can show me how to use it."

"Wrap it up again," she said. "We'd better get out of here."

They went down the stairs and out the front door, locking it behind them.

NINE

Nick's paranoia was in full bloom on the train back to Washington. His eyes never stopped moving, searching for any sign of the man who had attacked them in Branmore's house. He saw nothing out of the ordinary.

They picked up their car at the station and drove out to Virginia. Elizabeth and Stephanie were waiting for them in Elizabeth's office. Nick had the sword in his hand, inconspicuous under the cloth wrapping.

"You actually found the sword," Elizabeth said. "I don't believe it."

"How can you be certain it's the right one?" Stephanie asked.

"Trust me, it's the right one," Selena said. "All you need do is look at it. Masamune's swords are unmistakable."

Then Nick told Elizabeth about finding Branmore's head on his desk.

"You have to be kidding me," Elizabeth said.

"I wish I was."

"Did you touch anything when you were in the house?"

Nick looked at her.

"Oh, shit. I know where you're going. Fingerprints, right?"

"When they find the body, they're going to blanket that house with forensics teams. When your prints turn up, the NYPD is going to be very interested in talking with you."

"We didn't kill him."

"Of course not, but it could be a problem convincing them. Why is it every time you go somewhere I end up doing damage control?"

"Just lucky, I guess."

"All right. I'll see what I can do."

"Let's see the sword," Stephanie said.

Nick handed the sword to Selena.

"You show them."

"I'm almost certain no woman has ever drawn this blade," Selena said.

"Then you'll be the first."

Selena was highly skilled in martial arts. Her main study was in Korean *Kuk Sul Won*, but she was equally adept in Tae Kwon Do and an esoteric sword fighting form of Tai Chi. To hold Masamune's fabled weapon was like a gift from the gods.

She undid the wrapping and set it aside. The sword and scabbard made a perfect, graceful curve. Selena took a deep breath and moved away from Nick and the others.

She held the sword and scabbard at her side. With a quick movement she stepped back, knees bent, one foot planted at an angle behind her. At the same time she drew the blade, dropping the scabbard on the carpet. The sword came out of its sheath with a whisper, shining in the sunlight streaming through the office windows. She held it upright in front of her in both hands, ready to strike.

"Whoa," Nick said.

Selena moved in rapid sequence through an eight-sided series of movements mimicking the thrusts and parries of battle, the sword a blur. She ended with the blade once again held upright in front of her, ready to strike.

A yellow tennis ball lay in a tray on Elizabeth's desk. She used it to strengthen her hands and relax tension in her fingers.

"Elizabeth," Selena said. "Throw that tennis ball at me."

"Throw it at you? Are you serious?"

"Of course. Throw it as hard as you can."

"This should be interesting," Stephanie said.

"You asked for it," Elizabeth said. "I should warn you, I've got a mean arm."

She picked up the ball.

"Ready?"

Selena nodded. Elizabeth hurled the ball. The blade flashed and cut it in half. The two halves dropped to the floor.

"Holy shit," Nick said.

Selena's face broke into a wide grin.

"Sharp, isn't it? That's one of the ways you know it's a true Masamune."

"I can't believe you did that," Nick said.

Selena bent and picked up the scabbard, then re-sheathed the sword. She sat down, flushed with pleasure, holding it across her lap.

"What happens next, Director?" Nick asked.

"We're supposed to turn the sword over to Nobuyasu. But I'm beginning to wonder if he has something to do with these deaths."

"I thought we said it wasn't to his advantage."

"That was before someone killed Branmore's son. The only common factor in the murders is the sword. The only link to the sword is Nobuyasu."

"The only link we know of," Selena said.

"It doesn't make sense to me that it would be Nobuyasu," Nick said. "The proof is right there in Selena's lap. He hired us to find the sword. Why would he interfere? I don't trust him, but I don't think it's him."

"The man you saw in Branmore's house was Japanese. If Nobuyasu isn't behind these murders, who is?"

"It would have to be someone from Japan who knows about the sword and wants to keep it away from Nobuyasu."

"We're missing something," Selena said.

"What do you mean?" Elizabeth asked.

"What I mean is that we keep circling the same issue. There's something we don't know, some piece of information we don't have. Why is this sword important enough to kill for? Yes it's valuable, and yes it's an important cultural artifact, but cutting off someone's head?"

"You think there's something we don't know about it ?"

"I don't know, but putting Branmore's head on his desk sends a message."

"If it's a message, who is it for?"

"Maybe it's for us," Stephanie said.

"How about Nobuyasu?" Nick said.

"Why him?"

"Why not? Who else is involved? If someone sent me a message like that, I'd think long and hard about the implications."

"Such as?" Elizabeth asked.

"Such as, that could be *my* head," Nick said. "Or the head of someone I care about. That if I kept looking for the sword, it could happen to me."

"What if you had already found the sword?" Selena said.

"Then the message would be to hand it over, or else."

"I wonder what Nobuyasu will say when we tell him we have it?" Elizabeth said.

"You think we should give it to him?" Nick said.

"I'm not sure."

"What about Branmore, and those people who died in the fire at the nursing home? Do we give that up? Let it go? It doesn't feel right."

"Nick's right, Elizabeth," Selena said. "We can't simply hand it over and forget about it. Like it or not, we've landed in the middle of something that goes beyond recovering a cultural treasure. We have an obligation to find out what's going on."

"How do you propose that we do that?" Elizabeth asked.

"We have to go to the source."

"The source?"

Selena nodded. "Japan."

"You want to take the sword to Japan?"

"I didn't say that. That wouldn't be a good idea. I think we need to put it where no one can get to it until we find out what's going on."

"I know the perfect place," Stephanie said.

TEN

Sora Tanaka was a powerful man within his organization, the largest of the four principal yakuza families in Japan. Tanaka was a *wakagashira*, an underboss, responsible for operations on the West Coast of the U. S. mainland. It was an important job, and Tanaka took it seriously.

He was a short, hard man, sixty-four years old, broad shouldered and thick through the waist. His close cropped hair had once been black as the night sky, but had turned to gray as he aged, just as the tattoos that covered much of his body were beginning to lose their luster.

Tanaka's office was in California in Torrance, a city with a large Japanese presence. He sat behind a desk of lacquered wood in his office, looking out at the bustling crowds on Crenshaw Boulevard below and thinking about what to do about Saito, the man who had failed to retrieve the sword in New York.

Failure always had consequences. Saito had correctly offered to make up for his failure through the ritual of *yubitsume.* But having him cut off a digit of his little finger in an act of apology, though personally satisfying, would not solve the problem. If Tanaka could not successfully retrieve the ancient weapon, he would be the one bowing to the *oyabun* back in Kobe and taking up the knife to atone.

Failure to produce the desired results was unacceptable. It made him appear weak, and that was not tolerable. Tanaka had many enemies who would be happy to see him removed from his position, men who wanted to take his place, men who had little regard for the old traditions of respect.

These were men Tanaka held in contempt, but he could not afford to show weakness in front of them. There was only one possible course of action. He must succeed in bringing the sword back to Japan.

Saito had reported seeing the two Americans come out of Branmore's building carrying something wrapped in brown cloth, a package long enough and of the correct shape to be the sword. It was logical to assume Masamune's sword was now in their possession. They would contact Nobuyasu and hand it over to him. Tanaka would have to do something before the transfer took place.

Extreme violence was an integral way of life in the clan. Tanaka had hoped more violence could be avoided, but there didn't seem to be a choice. The Americans wouldn't give up the sword voluntarily. A man of violence was required for the assignment. He would use Saito, give him a chance to redeem himself.

Tanaka was sure Saito would never live to see thirty. He had a tendency to over react, with bad results for those who had gotten his attention. More than once, his temper had nearly cost him his life. One day it would be his undoing, but for now he was perfect for the plan forming in Tanaka's mind.

Nobuyasu was off-limits for the present. Killing him had been specifically forbidden. Tanaka thought that was a mistake. If Nobuyasu was eliminated, it would make it that much easier to retrieve the sword. The oyabun was worried that eliminating such a high profile target would create problems for the clan, problems with the police, with the government. The oyabun was getting old, but for now he was still the supreme boss.

There was no such limit regarding the Americans. Saito would be operating in the territory of the Eastern boss, Watanabe. Tanaka saw no reason to tell him about Saito's mission. The men were unfriendly rivals. Watanabe was insufferable. He would stick his nose in where it didn't belong and screw things up.

Tanaka picked up his phone.

ELEVEN

Hinata Saito stood naked in front of the full-length mirror mounted on the wall of his bedroom, admiring his body. The upper half of his muscular chest, his shoulders, and his arms down to the elbows were covered with brilliantly colored tattoos. They had been applied in the old way, with needles of steel and bamboo. He flexed his muscles and posed, turning back and forth in front of the mirror.

His large organ had not been tattooed. Few could handle the pain involved, but it was something he was considering for the future. The whores would find it impossible to resist, though they didn't seem to have any problems with it now, except to remark on the size.

A fierce demon in red and black and white with sharp teeth and tusks glared from his right arm, a depiction of an *Oni*. Oni were terrible demons who loved to feast on human flesh. The tattoo identified Saito as an enforcer of the rules of behavior. It also symbolized punishment, something Saito was experienced at providing to those who failed to meet their obligations to the clan.

On his left arm was an angry Samurai, sword raised, fierce-eyed, ready to attack. Saito believed he was descended from samurai forebears. The tattoo was both a warning and a demand for respect.

His back was still bare, but Saito was planning on getting a dragon. He hadn't decided which color to choose, and a tattoo that large would take several weeks to heal. He needed to put it off until he was sure there was enough time between assignments.

Saito was tall for a Japanese, a handsome man with fine, almost feminine features, and full, black hair. He was skilled in kendo and the traditional use of swords. He'd been looking forward to exercising with Masamune's mystical blade before he brought it to Los Angeles, but then the Americans had surprised him. Thinking about their unworthy hands defiling the ancient blade made his humiliation even more painful.

His cell phone buzzed where it lay on the unmade bed. The room was heavy with the odor of sex. An hour before, the bed had been occupied by a big-breasted blonde waitress he sometimes brought to his apartment. He'd sent her away as soon as he was done with her. Saito picked up the phone and looked at the display.

Tanaka. Shit.

"Yes, boss."

"I have an assignment for you. Do not fuck it up. You understand? I'm giving you another chance."

"Yes, boss, thank you. What must I do?"

"The people who have the sword are in Virginia. Go there, and retrieve it."

"Yes, boss. Where are they?"

"I will send you the location after this call. You need to be careful. These people are skilled. Do not underestimate them."

Fucking Americans, they don't know anything. Tanaka's getting to be like an old woman.

"Yes, boss."

"Saito. I can hear your thoughts. I'm serious, do not underestimate them. You understand?"

"Yes, boss."

"Do whatever you have to do, but get that sword. Your debt will be eliminated."

"Yes, boss. Thank you. I will not fail."

"Good, Saito. I count on you. Succeed, and you will be rewarded. Do you have questions?"

"Only one, boss. What if it's necessary to kill them?"

"You have permission. Do not get caught."

Tanaka broke the connection.

TWELVE

Elizabeth was thinking about Nobuyasu when her private line signaled a call from Clarence Hood. Hood was Director of the CIA, but Washington rumors said he wasn't long for the job. He was old school, unafraid to do whatever was required to keep the country safe. Elizabeth was surprised he was still at the helm of the Agency, since his views were almost opposite to those of the man currently in the White House.

Elizabeth had exposed the previous director as a traitor years before, when Hood had been deputy director. Their friendship had evolved to the point where they'd become intimate, something Elizabeth had thought no longer possible at her stage of life. Recently the relationship had cooled. Elizabeth wasn't certain where it was going. Whatever happened, there was deep affection between them.

When the Project disbanded, Hood had convinced President Hopkins that he'd be a fool to lose the expertise and experience of Elizabeth and her team. The Project was gone in its old form, but had been reconstituted under the shadowy umbrella of the CIA as an independent covert unit. She and the team could be called upon if needed, but the president was off the hook if something went wrong. Langley would take the heat.

She could still call on government resources if she needed to. She avoided that as much as possible, since she had to go through Langley to do it. Dealing with Langley's bureaucracy was a nightmare on the best of days. Selena was providing funding for the group until income from clients caught up with the overhead. Elizabeth thanked God for the day Selena had walked into her office, asking her to find the people who had murdered her beloved uncle.

Elizabeth wasn't comfortable about the quasi-official relationship with Langley, but she'd decided it was acceptable as long as Hood was director. It provided a modicum of governmental protection. When Hood was inevitably replaced, she'd reconsider.

"Good morning, Clarence."

"Hello, Elizabeth. I'm afraid your team has gotten itself in the middle of something again."

Elizabeth felt a flush of pleasure when she heard the soft, southern tones of his voice. Hood was Virginia born and raised.

"Oh?"

"Nick and Selena were recently in New York."

It wasn't a question.

"This is about Branmore, isn't it?"

"If you mean the man who was found in his home with his head cut off, yes, it's about him."

"It's a complicated story," Elizabeth said.

"It always is when you're concerned. Please tell me your people weren't responsible for Branmore's death."

"Of course they weren't. You know better than that."

"I had to ask, for the record. Nick and Selena's fingerprints are all over the crime scene. When the NYPD pulled up the prints, it triggered a red flag here at Langley. Lucas brought it to my attention."

Lucas Monroe was the director of clandestine operations at Langley. He was also Stephanie's husband.

Hood continued. "I got the New York cops to stand down. You won't be getting any unpleasant visits from their detectives."

"Thank you, Clarence. I'm glad to hear it."

"I need to know why Nick and Selena were in Branmore's house."

"They were looking for a sword."

"A sword? What kind of sword? Why were they looking for it?"

Elizabeth told him about Nobuyasu and the commission to find the Honjo Masamune.

"Atagi Nobuyasu? The man who controls a big piece of Japanese manufacturing?"

"The same."

"Nobuyasu has been on our radar for some time. He belongs to an extreme right wing group called Black Swan. His politics make Genghis Khan look like a liberal. He's mixed up with the yakuza and is backing their candidate for prime minister in the election that's coming up."

"Go on."

"I'm sure you did your due diligence before you took a commission from him. What did you discover?"

"That he's one of the richest men in Japan and involved in an extremist group within the conservative party."

"He stays hidden behind the scenes, but he's pulling a lot of strings. If his candidate wins the election, Japan is going to go hard right. That will threaten stability in the region. Nobuyasu is acting for the keiretsu. They want to rebuild the military, with the ultimate aim of counteracting Chinese and Russian influence. They want to bring back the good old days of empire. It's a business greed cloaked as patriotism. They want nukes and a standing army, all of which is forbidden by their constitution."

"I know there's a lot of agitation in Japan to change the constitution. They're worried about China. I can't say I blame them."

"If Nobuyasu's candidate wins, they'll get their army. They'll also get a dramatic increase in crime. The keiretsu and the yakuza have formed an unofficial alliance. It could shift the balance of power in Japan. The yakuza are well organized and completely ruthless. It's legal to be a member of a yakuza organization. The leaders are good at manipulating public opinion to make it look as though they're valuable members of the community. When something happens, they use it as a public relations opportunity."

"When something happens?"

"I'll give you an example. During the last big earthquake they showed up right away with tons of food and supplies, days before the government managed to get its act together. Actions like that go a long way toward gaining popular support."

"I've been wondering about Nobuyasu. I had a feeling he wasn't quite what he appeared to be," Elizabeth said. "Now you've confirmed it."

"We were watching Branmore. He was using his construction business to bring drugs into the country. We knew he was doing it, but no one was able to come up with the evidence to prove it. The police think that's what got him killed."

"When Nick and Selena were in Branmore's house, the killer was still there. He knocked them down and ran out of the house. Nick said he was Japanese. We think he was there looking for the sword."

"You think Branmore was killed because he had an old sword? Not drugs?"

"Yes, I do. His father was the one who brought the sword here from Japan after the war. He was murdered a few days ago. Someone burned down the rest home where he was living, along with dozens of innocent people. I don't think it was a coincidence."

"Is that why Nick and Selena went to New York?"

"We found out Branmore had a son. I sent Nick and Selena to talk to him and see if he remembered anything about the sword. They were posing as reporters. Branmore thought they were going to interview him for an article in the New York Times and made an appointment. They found the door unlocked and discovered the body. The place had been ransacked. Then they heard someone moving around upstairs. After the killer knocked them down, they searched the rest of the house and found the sword."

"You didn't tell me they found it."

"I'm telling you now."

"Do you plan to give it to Nobuyasu?"

"Not yet, not after what you just told me. I want to send Nick and Selena to Japan first and see what they can find out."

"Ah."

"Ah? Every time you say that, I wonder what you're thinking."

"I'm thinking we have a mutual interest in finding out more about Nobuyasu. How are you planning to proceed in Japan?"

"We haven't discussed it yet."

"You need help. If you go in there cold, no one will tell you anything. Selena may speak Japanese, but it's going to take more than that."

"What do you have in mind?"

"You need someone over there who can open doors and provide you with information. The head of the Public Security Intelligence Agency is an acquaintance of mine. His name's Daichi Yamamoto. I'll call him and ask for his help, plus I can provide credentials that will give Nick and Selena credibility and a degree of protection.

Yamamoto believes in a democratic Japan.
If he thinks you'll help him pin something
on Nobuyasu, he'll do everything he can for
you."

"That's an excellent idea, Clarence. I
appreciate the help. But I don't think you
should mention the sword to him, not yet.
As soon as someone in Japan knows we
have it, they'll want it back. We'd lose any
chance of finding out what's really going
on."

"He's going to want to know why you're
there."

"Let him have part of it. Tell him
Nobuyasu hired us to find the sword. Tell
him we suspect he wants to keep it for
himself, instead of doing the right thing and
handing it over to the National Museum.
Tell him Nick and Selena want to go to
Japan to look for leads. He doesn't have to
know we found it."

"He might buy that. Let me know when
you're ready and I'll call him."

After Hood ended the call, Elizabeth got
up and went over to the coffee station. She
made a fresh cup and returned to her desk.

Nick and Selena were coming in soon.
She thought about what Hood had said. It
would make things easier if someone as
powerful as the director of Japan's CIA was
in their corner, but she was under no illusion
that her interests and Yamamoto's
necessarily coincided.

She sat back in her chair and thought
about how things had changed since
President Hopkins had disbanded the

Project. Ronnie was off in Arizona, studying to be a healer in the Navajo tradition. Lamont was down in Florida, not doing much of anything, as far as she knew. She missed the daily interaction with everyone. The team meetings had always been one of the highlights of her day, even when someone was arguing with her.

She wondered if she ought to call Ronnie and Lamont back. Neither one of them spoke Japanese, so they wouldn't be much use in Japan. Besides, there was no reason to expect trouble, not if Yamamoto gave them his blessing. Nonetheless, something nagged at the back of her mind, something she couldn't put her finger on.

A memory of her father surfaced.

Judge Harker had been the kind of man people told stories about. He was the sort of judge the innocent wanted and the guilty feared, hard and fair. Elizabeth was sure he must have made mistakes while he was on the bench, but she'd never heard him talk about them.

One day she'd asked him how he decided if someone was guilty or not, when the evidence seemed unclear or contradictory, or when it wasn't up to a jury. She must have been about twelve years old at the time, back in Colorado, where she'd grown up on the front range. It had been late spring. Daffodils were blooming in the front yard and the snow was retreating to the high country. She could almost smell the clean, crisp, Rocky Mountain air as the memory swept over her.

"It's a little hard to explain how I do it," he'd said. *"There are times when a decision can go either way. Lawyers are awfully good at twisting the law the way that works best for their client or for the prosecution. Sometimes an innocent person can be convicted."*

"Isn't the law supposed to protect the innocent? Isn't that what the justice system is supposed to do?"

The judge laughed. "Theoretically, yes. But the law is subject to interpretation. Justice is supposed to be blind when she weighs the scales, but a good lawyer can tip it in the wrong direction."

"That's awful."

"That's the nature of the beast, Elizabeth. Humans make mistakes and the law is not perfect. My job is to make sure no one puts his thumb on the scales."

"So how do you decide?"

"I trust my intuition."

"Intuition?"

"It's a feeling, difficult to describe. Sometimes, I'm looking at a man whose life is in the balance. Maybe he's going to go to prison for a long time, and if he does, I know he will never be the same. He's been accused of a crime. Did he do it? That's the big question. Sometimes it's completely obvious, but sometimes it isn't. That's when intuition comes into play. It's what people call a gut feeling. Something inside tells me what to do."

"Like a voice in your head?"

"Once in a while, I've had that happen. Mostly it's a feeling I'm about to make a bad decision or a good one. If a jury has already found him guilty, it comes down to a question of the sentence. Sometimes I don't have a choice because of the crime. When I do, I ask myself if he deserves leniency. That's when my intuition comes into play."

"Is it like when you think something bad might happen but you don't really have a good reason for thinking like that, and then something bad does happen?"

"It's exactly like that, sweetie. Have you ever felt like that?"

"Uh, huh. Remember in December, when Suzy Miller fell through the ice? I had a bad feeling right before it happened. She almost died."

"Then you have the gift. A strong intuition will help you through your whole life. You should learn to trust it. It takes practice, and sometimes you'll make a mistake. But in the end it's always the right thing to trust your instincts."

"Penny for your thoughts."

Stephanie's voice startled Elizabeth out of her reverie.

"I was thinking about something my father said to me, years ago, about intuition."

"What brought that on?"

"I'm not sure," Elizabeth said, "but I'm starting to wonder if this trip to Japan is really a good idea."

THIRTEEN

Saito figured there were two possible locations where he might find the sword. One was the home of the Americans he'd seen leaving Branmore's place in New York with the sword. The second was a large house in Virginia where they worked. Either one presented problems.

Saito wished he'd never heard of the damn sword. If those two hadn't shown up when they did, he would've found it and everything would have been fine. Instead, his future in the clan was in jeopardy. Failure to accomplish the task given to him was not acceptable. It would take more than the loss of part of a finger to make up for it. To make sure there were no problems this time, he'd called in two men from Los Angeles. He'd picked them because of their comfort with violence.

Hozumi Ito was a small, wiry man, small even for a Japanese, but the chip on his shoulder was big enough for someone much larger. Ito always needed to prove he was better than men bigger than he was. He could explode into extreme rage at the slightest insult, real or imagined. The man radiated nervous energy. Even when he was sitting, he always seemed to be in motion. The key to using him effectively was to keep him focused and sober. He liked to drink black label scotch, but he wasn't fussy. Once Ito got into the liquor, all bets were off.

Although he was careful never to say it out loud, Saito thought Ito resembled nothing so much as an angry monkey. Saito had seen him in action when he let out his rage. It had convinced him never to get on Ito's shit list.

On the surface, Kenki Nakamura was almost the exact opposite of Ito. He was a few inches short of six feet tall, broad shouldered and calm, with the kind of bland, smooth face people never remembered. In the old days, Nakamura would have been called a twelve bottle man. He could drink sake for hours with little apparent effect. Like Ito, he contained a capacity for violence that was unusual, even within the culture of the yakuza.

Both men were experienced. Both were excellent shots and were vicious with the knife. With Ito and Nakamura backing him up, Saito would have no problem in any confrontation.

The three men were parked down the street from the building where the two Americans lived. Saito had not decided which location would be best to target, but he was leaning toward Virginia. The Americans worked for someone else. The logical thing would be to take the sword to the boss. That's what he would do. Keeping such a valuable weapon at home didn't make sense, but Americans didn't think like other people. The sword could be right there in front of him. Plus, there would be more people to deal with at their headquarters.

Where were they most vulnerable? How could he guarantee that when he made his move, the sword would be in the right place? He wouldn't get more than one chance at it.

Tanaka had told him the Americans should not be underestimated, but Saito dismissed that as the nervousness of an old man. He and his men were skilled in the arts of intimidation and murder. What possible problem could these soft foreigners present against the three of them?

Soft they might be, but Saito knew the best way to succeed required planning. This was the second day he'd been watching the building. He'd learned that the Americans lived on the top floor. There was a guard and security desk on the ground floor. Cameras covered the entrance to the building, the garage, and a service entrance in the back.

The morning before, he'd observed the woman and a companion come out of the building with a double stroller and two small children. It was logical to assume the children were hers. The companion was probably some sort of caretaker.

"Look, boss," Nakamura said. "There they are."

A car came out of the garage, a large black SUV. The man and the woman were in the front seat.

"Get down," Saito said.

The three ducked down out of sight. The next time he looked, the car was disappearing around a corner.

"They're going to work," he said.

"What do you want to do, boss?" Ito asked.

A plan had been forming in Saito's mind.

"We have to check out their apartment. We get in and look for the sword. Somebody will be there to watch the children, maybe that woman we saw yesterday. She won't be a problem."

"What if the sword isn't there?"

"We'll have the children. The man will bring it to us. I'll threaten to kill the children if he calls the police."

Ito laughed. "Brilliant, boss. That should do it."

"If we find the sword, so much the better for them."

"What about the woman who's watching them?"

"She'll have seen us. We can't leave her around."

"Boss?" Ito said. "Can we play with her first?"

"Do you ever think about something besides sex?"

"Sometimes he thinks about getting drunk," Nakamura said.

"Are you making fun of me?" Ito said.

"What if I was?"

"Both of you, knock it off. There's a service alley in back of the building. We'll go in that way. Ito, if there's a camera, you take care of it. Nakamura, you have your picks?"

"Always, boss."

"You work the lock on the door. Okay, let's go."

They got out of the car and crossed the street to the alley that ran in back of Nick's building. No one was in sight. Several trash cans were lined up in a row beside a gray door in the back wall. A camera was positioned over the door. The way it faced, it hadn't seen them coming down the alley.

Ito took a small spray can from his pocket, reached up and blotted out the lens on the camera. With a little luck, anyone watching would assume the camera had failed. If someone came looking, they would be unpleasantly surprised.

Nakamura had the door open in less than a minute. They entered and closed it behind them. They were in the basement of the building. The room was dim, but enough light came from somewhere up front to show them which way to go.

Saito heard music that got louder as they neared the source of the light. Someone was humming along with a song being played on a radio. They came up to two large boilers. Saito held up his hand. The light and the music was somewhere to the left of where he stood.

He peered around the edge of the boiler. A gray-haired man in blue overalls and a blue shirt sat on a stool at a workbench soldering something in front of him. A thin wisp of smoke rose into the air over the work. Saito slipped a sock filled with lead buckshot from his jacket, and moved toward him. The janitor sensed something and started to turn around.

"What..."

Saito brought the leaded sock down on the man's temple with a savage blow. He went down without a sound. There was a large dent on the side of his head. The stool clattered on the floor. A set of keys on a ring hung from the janitor's belt. Saito took them and kicked the unconscious man in his stomach.

Fucking Americans.

"Come on."

Ito and Nakamura followed Saito to a stairwell and elevator. He pressed the button for the elevator. Nothing happened. Then he noticed a lock by the button. He tried several of the janitor's keys before he found the right one. He turned the key in the lock and was rewarded by the sound of the elevator descending to the basement. The doors opened.

"Going up," he said.

FOURTEEN

Anna Montalbano was in the children's room. She'd gotten the twins down for a nap when she heard the front door open.

They must've forgotten something.

She was about to go out of the room and suddenly stopped. Someone was talking. He wasn't speaking English. She thought maybe it was Japanese or Chinese. Whoever it was, he wasn't supposed to be there. That meant he was a threat to the children.

Anna had been working for Selena and Nick for several months. One day Selena had taken her aside. Early on, Selena had told her to call her by her first name.

"Anna, I'd like to talk with you about something."

"What about, Selena?"

"You don't really know much about Nick and myself, our history. I think it's time to fill you in."

"Okay. I'd like that. I admit, I've been curious."

Selena told her some of what she and Nick had done in the Project. She kept it general, but made sure Anna understood that they'd made some serious enemies over the years.

"That's why you and Nick carry guns?"

"I should've realized you would notice that."

"Pretty hard not to. I didn't want to pry. I know you both work for the government."

Selena didn't try to clarify the complex relationship she and Nick had with Langley and the White House.

"How do you feel about guns?"

"I'm not afraid of them, if that's what you mean. My father had a pistol. He taught me how to shoot. Guns don't bother me, as long as they're not pointed my way."

"That makes what I want to say to you easier. I'd like you to begin carrying a pistol. I'll arrange a permit. We have an indoor range where I work. You can practice there. Nick or I will show you some tricks."

"Are you worried about the children? Has someone threatened them?"

"I always worry about the children. No one has specifically threatened them, but it's always possible someone might in the future. Nick and I have talked this over. We think you do a wonderful job and we want you to keep working with us. We'd feel better if you were armed. The chances are small that anything would ever happen, but if it did, we'd like to know you could protect the twins and yourself if you had to."

"This is Washington. You can actually get a permit?"

"Yes. What do you think?"

"I feel like I'm in some kind of a spy movie or something."

Selena waited.

"You really think the twins might be at risk?"

Selena noticed that Anna said nothing about the fact she might also be at risk, since she was constantly with the twins.

"It's always possible."

"I couldn't live with myself if something happened to Jason and Katrina," Anna said. "If you really think I need a gun to protect them, I'm game."

Nick had given Anna a Sig-sauer P229 in .40 Smith & Wesson. She kept it concealed in a penny pack she wore on her belt. Listening to the strange voices in the front room, she took it out. Quietly, she moved to the door of the room and closed it. Still holding the pistol, she dragged a chest of toys across the door to block it. Then she took out her cell phone and thumbed a preprogrammed emergency signal that went to Nick and Selena's phones.

Nick picked up. Anna could hear road noises in the background. Nick was still in the car, driving to work.

"Anna. What's the matter?"

She kept her voice low.

"Someone's in the loft. Sounds like he's Japanese or Chinese, Asian anyway."

"Okay. Keep calm. We're about fifteen minutes out. I'm turning off now. We'll be back as quick as we can. Stay calm. Keep the line open."

"Okay."

"Keep the line open."

"I'm scared."

"You'll be all right. We're on our way. Stay calm."

Someone tried the door, pushing against the heavy toy chest.

"They're coming in," Anna said.

On the phone, Nick heard a noise as the door was shoved open. Someone shouted in Japanese. There was the sound of a shot. Then loud noises and shouts. He could make out Anna screaming and someone yelling in Japanese. Then someone picked up the phone.

"Anna?"

"We want the sword," a man's voice said in heavily accented English.

"Who are you?"

"We want the sword," the man said again. "If you don't bring it to us, we will kill the girl. Then we will kill the children. Such a shame, so young. If you call the police, everyone will die. You understand, American?"

Nick felt rage, then an adrenaline rush. Every sense came alive. He was weaving through traffic, doing eighty miles an hour.

The twins. He'll hurt the twins. Son of a bitch.

"Yeah, I understand."

"Nick," Selena said. "What's happening?"

"Bring the sword, or they die."

"I have to go get it. It's not in the loft. You understand? It's in Virginia. It will take time for me to go there."

"You have one hour," the voice said. Then the connection was broken.

"Nick," Selena said.

"Someone's in the loft. He's after the sword. He says he'll kill Anna and the kids if I don't bring him the sword."

Selena's heart began pounding in her chest.

"What are we going to do?"

It was one of the things he loved about Selena. She didn't panic. Not so you'd notice, anyway.

"We're going back to the loft. We can't call the cops. He said he'd kill everyone if we did. I believe him."

"You're not going to give him the sword?"

"No. It wouldn't do any good. He can't let anyone live. There's more than one of them. We have to kill them or put them out of action."

"Anna. What happened to her?"

"I don't know. We'll worry about that later."

They crossed the river into the city.

FIFTEEN

Nick drove into the garage and parked. They got out of the car and checked their pistols.

"How do you want to do it?" Selena asked.

"We have a couple of advantages. One is that they don't know we're here yet. We have a little time."

"You said a couple of advantages. What's the other one?"

"They can't be familiar with the building. They'll expect us to come up the regular way, either the stairs or the elevator from the lobby. They won't know about the service elevator. We'll use that to get to the loft."

Each floor of the building had one unit. Each unit had two separate means of access, although no one who didn't live there would know that. The front door was reached by the main elevator or staircase. In the back of each unit was a small service elevator, used mostly by catering services on special occasions. Inside the loft, the door to the elevator could be mistaken for a pantry or closet. The entrance to the service elevator was in the basement.

"And when we get there?"

He held up his pistol.

"That's when all that practice with these pays off. Makes me glad we installed the lasers. We can't mess around with these guys. I don't know how many there are, but we take them down. All of them. We can't give them a chance to respond."

"A lot could go wrong."

"I know. But I don't see what else we can do. Negotiation isn't going to work."

"What if they're holding the twins?"

Nick looked at her. "You can't think about that. Shoot past them. Shoot to kill."

"Oh, Nick."

"I know. Come on, let's go."

They entered the basement through a door in the garage, walked past the elevator and saw the body of the janitor.

Nick bent down and felt for a pulse. He looked up and shook his head.

"Bastards," Selena said. "His granddaughter was graduating from college next week."

They went to the other end of the building where the service elevator was located.

"When the door opens up there, we don't know where they'll be," Nick said. "With a little luck, they'll be all the way in the front and they might not hear us. If that's the way it turns out, we move front until we have a shot. Worst case, someone's there when we come out of the elevator. We take him out. It would be better if we can do it without noise. If not, do your best. We'll have to move fast. You ready?"

She nodded. Nick called for the elevator. The door opened, and they stepped in. Nick punched the button for their floor.

The elevator rose slowly toward the top of the building.

SIXTEEN

Saito finished bandaging the wound on Nakamura's chest where Anna's bullet had hit him. The .40 caliber hollow point had made a real mess. Nakamura was unconscious. He'd lost a lot of blood.

The twins were screaming. Saito was tempted to shoot them to stop the noise. Anna lay crumpled in a heap on the floor. Ito had charged past as Anna shot Nakamura and punched her as hard as he could. She'd gone down and hadn't moved since.

"Ito. Wake the woman. Get her to shut up these damn kids."

"Yes, boss."

He went over to where Anna lay and knelt down beside her. He reached out and pinched her cheek, then slapped her. She groaned.

"Wake up, bitch. Come on, wake up. If you don't, you'll wish you were dead."

Anna opened her eyes. Her head hurt. She looked into Ito's eyes. She'd never seen eyes like that. There didn't seem to be anything behind them, no life. They were like empty black spots in his head.

He slapped her again.

"Get up."

She struggled to her knees, then leaned against the wall, dizzy. She heard the twins howling.

Ito prodded her with his gun.

"Make them shut up, or I'll do it for you. You understand? Make them quiet, or else."

"All right," Anna said. "Don't hurt them."

Ito slapped her.

"You don't talk except to get them to shut up. Understand?"

Anna wanted to kick him in the balls, but she knew she'd never get away with it. The other one, the one she hadn't shot, was watching her. She nodded.

Ito shoved her toward the playpen.

"Get going."

She knelt down and began comforting the children. In a few moments their cries had turned to whimpers and occasional sobs. She heard the men talking in Japanese.

Saito looked at his watch.

"Another half hour. Then we kill one of the children. Or maybe the nanny."

"What are you going to do when the man shows up, boss?"

"I'm going to have him show me the sword. Then I'm going to kill him."

"What about the others?"

"Once we have the sword, we kill them too."

"Can I take the woman, first?"

"Idiot. There's no time for that."

Ito suddenly looked toward the back of the loft.

"I thought I heard something."

"There's no one else here."

"No, boss, I heard something."

"All right. Go check it out."

Ito moved toward the back, silent as a cat, moving along on the balls of his feet. His pistol was ready in his hand. Saito went into the room where Anna was sitting in the playpen with the children. Jason looked up at Saito and began to cry.

"Keep them quiet."

"You scare them. I can't help that," Anna said.

"They should be scared. If you…"

Whatever Saito was going to say was cut short by gunshots and a scream. He couldn't be sure, but he thought it was Ito that had cried out. He reached down and grabbed Katrina and held her against his chest. She began kicking and screaming and waving tiny fists in the air.

Saito waited, his pistol aimed at the door. A man's voice called out.

"You in the room. Come out, with your hands up."

"I have your child, American. I will kill it. Throw your gun where I can see it."

"You hurt my kid, you're a dead man."

"Very brave, when my gun is at your child's head. What will you do when I pull the trigger? Shoot me? I'm already dead. Throw your gun down or I kill it now."

"All right. I'll throw the gun. I have the sword. That's what you want, isn't it? Let me see that my kids are all right and I'll give it to you."

"First, the gun," Saito said.

A black automatic clattered on the wood floor in front of the room.

"Get up," Saito said to Anna. He backed away from the playpen. "Take the other child and get in front of me. Try something, I'll kill you both."

Anna picked up Jason and got out of the playpen.

"Move." Saito gestured with the gun. "Tell him you're coming out. Tell him you're both dead if he tries anything."

"Nick," Anna called. "I'm coming out with Jason. He says he'll kill us if you do anything."

"He can see my gun. I'm unarmed," Nick said.

I hope he's lying.

"Let me see you, American. Hands in the air, where I can see them."

"All right. I'm coming. My hands are in the air."

Nick came into view in the doorway. His hands were in the air.

"Where is the sword?" Saito asked.

"I set it down. You said hands in the air."

"Go," Saito said to Anna.

She came out of the room, holding Jason, and moved over next to Nick. Down the hall, Selena waited with her gun held in front of her in both hands. The red eye of a laser shone under the barrel

"You all right, Anna?" Nick said.

"I'm fine. One of them is wounded. In there."

Saito started out of the room, holding Katrina high against his chest. Selena shot him through the neck. The bullet cut through his brainstem, severing the signals from his brain, preventing him from pulling the trigger. Nick snatched Katrina away as Saito fell to the floor.

He held his daughter close and rocked her.

"Okay, sweetie, it's okay. I've got you now."

Katrina lifted a tear stained face to Nick and reached up to touch him.

"Dada."

Selena came up to where Saito lay dead on the floor, still holding her pistol in both hands. She looked down at him and nudged him with her foot.

"Bastard."

"I'm going back into the kitchen," Nick said. "The other one might still be alive."

SEVENTEEN

Ito opened his eyes. What had happened? His chest hurt, a lot. His shirt was wet with something warm, sticky. Then he remembered. The woman with the children had shot him. A woman!

A large, angry man stood nearby, towering over him and looking down at Ito where he lay on the hard floor.

The American.

"Who are you? Who sent you here?"

Ito spoke English but he wasn't going to admit it. Where was Saito?

Nick kicked Ito in the side. He shouted in pain.

"Talk, you bastard. Who sent you?"

"No… English."

Nick kicked him again. "I think you speak English just fine."

Selena said, "Nick, I don't think that's going to work. Let me talk to him."

"He's yakuza. Look at his tattoos. He's not going to say anything unless he's forced to."

"Let me try."

Nick stepped back.

"Go ahead."

Selena knelt down by Ito and began speaking to him in Japanese.

"You are badly wounded. You've lost a lot of blood. You will die here if you do not tell us what we want to know."

Ito was stunned by this woman's perfect Japanese. But Americans were soft. They were bluffing.

"I need a doctor." He coughed blood. "You have to take me to a doctor."

"A doctor? Why would I do that? If you want to see a doctor, answer my questions."

"You cannot let me die."

"Of course I can let you die."

"Selena, wait a second."

Nick grabbed Ito's feet and dragged him across the floor to where he could see Saito's body lying down the hall. His eyes went wide open.

Selena saw the movement.

"Oh, you see your friend?" Selena said. "I killed him, so sorry. You threatened to kill my children. I don't care if you die. Unless you tell me what I want to know, we'll let you bleed to death before we call anyone. My husband wants to hurt you. Your death will not be pleasant."

Ito looked at her eyes. They were the most unusual eyes he'd ever seen, a deep, violet color. Her face was hard and fierce, like an angry *kami*. Looking at her, he knew she meant what she'd said.

"This is your last chance," Selena said. "Why did you come here?"

"The sword," Ito said. "We came to get the sword."

"Who sent you?"

"Orders... we were ordered."

"Who gave the order?"

"Tanaka. Tanaka gave the order."

"Who is Tanaka?"

"He is…boss. *Wakagashira.*
You…understand?

"Yes. Where is this man?"

Ito was dizzy. The room was beginning to spin. Selena shook him.

"Where is he?"

Ito's eyes closed. "He's lost too much blood," Selena said. "We're not going to get anything else out of him."

"What did he say?"

"They were ordered to get the sword by their boss, someone named Tanaka."

"Did he say where we could find Tanaka?"

"No."

Nick took out his phone.

"I'll call Harker."

He spoke for a few moments and ended the call.

"She's sending someone. Let's try to keep him alive until they get here."

Selena had been kneeling next to Ito. Now she stood.

"Too late. He's gone. Anna said there's one more, in the kids' room, wounded."

"What a mess."

"Thank God for Anna."

"Where is she?"

"In the living room with the kids, away from this."

"She has to be pretty shook up."

"Let's go talk to her."

Nick looked down at Ito's body.

He got up and walked back to find the man Anna had shot. Nakamura was propped up against a wall, his chest covered with blood, dead.

In my home, Nick thought. Then, *I hate this.*

EIGHTEEN

Nick and Selena sat on the couch near Elizabeth's desk. Stephanie was at her console nearby. Nick finished telling Elizabeth what had happened.

"It's too bad he died before he could tell you more," Elizabeth said.

"At least we have a name," Selena said, "and we know this Tanaka person is an under boss. That's an important position in the yakuza hierarchy, second only to the big boss, the *oyabun*."

"If we needed confirmation the yakuza are involved, we have it now," Elizabeth said. "It's unusual for these people to target children. It shows how badly they want to get their hands on the sword."

"I don't get it," Nick said. "Why go to these extremes? Branmore and his son are dead, along with all those people in that fire. They killed the old guy that took care of our building. He was just a bystander. I'm certain they would have killed Selena and me and our kids. Seems a little over the top."

"I can't figure it out either," Selena said. "For one thing, you could never let anyone know you had the sword. You couldn't sell it. It's a national treasure. For someone who's Japanese, that means a great deal."

"I don't think the yakuza give a damn about those kinds of things," Nick said.

"Maybe not. But it still doesn't make sense."

"Let me see what Freddie can dig up on Tanaka," Stephanie said. "Freddie?"

Yes, Stephanie?

"Have you been listening to the conversation?"

Of course.

"I'd like you to find out about this person named Tanaka."

I anticipated your request and have already done so. Would you like to hear what I have discovered?

Stephanie rolled her eyes. "Yes, Freddie. Please tell us what you have discovered."

Sora Tanaka is a high-ranking member of the largest yakuza clan, based in Kobe. He is currently in charge of clan operations on the West Coast of the United States. He lives in Los Angeles in the Little Tokyo historical district and directs operations from there. Would you like to hear about yakuza operations within the United States?

"Not right now, Freddie, thank you," Stephanie said.

Are you sure? It really is most interesting. Tanaka oversees an extensive network involving drugs, prostitution, and extortion.

"Not now, Freddie."

"If he's in Los Angeles, I can pay him a visit," Nick said. "If he sent them he must know why they want the sword."

"Probably," Elizabeth said. "But a man like that will be well guarded. He isn't going to surrender information without violence. That's not the best way to go about this."

"He won't be expecting me."

"After everything that happened, the twins need me here," Selena said. "I'm not going to LA. You can't take on the yakuza by yourself."

"I wasn't thinking of doing it by myself. I want Ronnie and Lamont to go with me."

NINETEEN

Atagi Nobuyasu lived in central Tokyo, in an exclusive area of luxury condos and large homes far beyond the reach of the average Japanese. The Imperial Palace was nearby. Some of the homes here dated back to the times of the daimyos and the samurai. It was one of these, situated within a walled compound with a large, carefully tended private garden, that Nobuyasu called home.

The building was traditional, as befitted a man who believed in restoring Japan's past. The floors were made of polished cypress and covered with tatami mats of the highest quality. *Yukumi shoji*, traditional sliding screens of paper that could be lifted to reveal a window, were a slight concession to modernity. They preserved the traditional look and allowed light to pass through, but the windows offered a barrier against the weather.

Stepping into Nobuyasu's home was like taking a journey into the heart of Japan's history. A beautiful entrance hall greeted the visitor, where visitors took off their shoes and stored them in a cabinet made for that purpose. No one wore shoes inside a Japanese home. The rest of the structure was slightly elevated above the level of the entrance. Tokyo often experienced heavy rains during the monsoon season. Raising the floor helped prevent flooding.

Various rooms inside were used for relaxation, preparing food, bathing, viewing the garden or the moon, sleeping and entertaining. There were no chairs, no Western furniture, only low tables and cushions. Sleeping futons were stored in cabinets during the day. It was a home that would have seemed familiar and comfortable to an upper-class Japanese from the seventeenth century.

Nobuyasu was a man of culture and taste, well acquainted with the many artistic traditions of Japan. He was especially fond of the art of bonsai.

Bonsai was much more than making a miniature of something that grew large in nature. A true masterpiece produced a complex feeling of emotion and appreciation that could only come from observing perfect balance and symmetry. Pride of place in his collection was a particularly nice example of a three hundred-year-old pine, a little under twelve inches tall. It had been created to form the illusion of a tree on a rocky cliff, the branches bent as though swept by winds.

The bonsai had been placed on a low table. Nobuyasu sat cross legged in front of it, contemplating its perfection. Usually, fifteen minutes in front of the tree was enough to restore his sense of harmony at the end of the day. But today was different. He couldn't stop thinking about Masamune's sword, and all of his thoughts were disturbing.

He knew Harker's people had found it. Why hadn't she called him? He couldn't ask for it without revealing that he'd been spying on her. That was the least of his concerns. Far more important was the involvement of the yakuza. That made everything more complicated. His informer in Kobe had reported that a yakuza operation had gone badly wrong in the United States, and that it involved the sword.

The yakuza were supposed to be allied with Nobuyasu, in support of the common goal to restore a powerful Japan. They were not supposed to know about Harker, or that Nobuyasu had hired her to find the sword. No one except a few people within Black Swan knew that. One of them could have gone to the yakuza. Or it could have been one of the people he'd assigned to keep an eye on the Americans.

Either way, he'd been betrayed.

Finding the traitor would take time, but Nobuyasu was patient. Sooner or later, the man's name would be revealed and a suitable punishment administered. In the meantime, he had to retrieve the sword.

Why hadn't Harker called? Before he did anything he needed to find out more about what had happened in America. Perhaps he needed to force the issue. Now that the sword had been located, it was only a question of time before it was in his hands.

One way or another, he would have it.

TWENTY

Ronnie Peete and Lamont Cameron stood in front of the new headquarters in Virginia.

"Fancy digs," Ronnie said.

"Nick said it was pretty nice. Like working in someone's country home."

"Yeah, someone named Rockefeller maybe."

Ronnie and Nick went back a long way. They'd first met in a Marine Recon unit years before. Ronnie was a stocky, wide shouldered man with a narrow waist, a full blooded Navajo. When the Project disbanded, he'd gone back to the reservation in Arizona to study with his uncle, one of the last traditional healers on the Reservation.

Lamont was a former Navy SEAL. Nick had recruited Lamont as he was about to complete his twenty years. They'd met during a joint mission in Iraq. He was whipcord lean, in the way an NFL wide receiver was lean, all muscle and speed. He'd lost some of the speed with injuries he'd gotten during his time with the Project, but he was tough as old iron.

The two friends climbed the steps and entered the foyer. Lamont looked at the sweeping staircase rising to the second floor of the building and whistled.

"Like I said, fancy."

Nick came out of the back of the house.

"Well I'll be damned," Nick said. "Look what the cat dragged in."

"Hey, Nick," Ronnie said.

Nick hugged each of them in turn.

"Man, it's good to see you guys."

Ronnie was wearing a bright Hawaiian shirt from his collection. Nick looked at him and shaded his eyes.

"Bright. I've missed those gaudy shirts of yours."

"This? This isn't gaudy. This shirt is a work of art. You really need to get educated, Nick."

"You're looking pretty good, " Lamont said. "Looks like being a dad agrees with you."

"They keep me busy, that's for sure. Come on in. The others are in the back."

Stephanie, Selena, and Elizabeth were waiting in Elizabeth's office.

"Hi, guys," Selena said.

She got up off the couch where she'd been sitting and hugged them. Stephanie followed suit. Elizabeth stood up behind her desk and gestured at the couch.

"Take a seat. I'm really glad to see both of you."

"Kind of like old times," Lamont said. He sat down on the couch next to a large orange cat and scratched it behind the ears.

"Hi, Burps."

Burps looked up and drooled, rumbling like a miniature truck. Ronnie sat down next to Lamont.

"So it's the Harker Group now," Ronnie said. "No more Project?"

"Not officially, no," Elizabeth said. "Things are a lot calmer now."

"I'll believe that when I see it," Lamont said. "If things are so calm, how come you called us?"

"It's a long story," Nick said.

"It always is."

"We've run into a little problem with the yakuza," Elizabeth said.

"The Japanese Mafia?" Ronnie said.

Elizabeth nodded. "That's right."

"Those guys are bad dudes," Lamont said. "You ever see Black Rain? Cool movie."

"I need to go out to LA to talk to one of their bosses," Nick said. "I figured you guys might like to come along as backup."

"You want us to help you talk to some Japanese Godfather?"

"More or less."

"I knew I should've stayed in Florida."

"What's going on, Nick?" Ronnie asked.

"It's about an old sword," Nick said.

"Oh, boy," Lamont said. "Every time we get mixed up with something old, things get real complicated. What is it, Excalibur?"

Nick laughed. "No, not Excalibur. It's a sword made by Japan's greatest sword smith, eight hundred years ago. For the Japanese, it's like Excalibur. They consider it a national treasure."

Elizabeth said, "The sword disappeared at the end of World War II. We were hired to find it. We did find it, but the yakuza want it. They came after Nick and Selena and their kids."

"Oh, oh," Lamont said. "That must've pissed you off. I'll bet that didn't work out too well for them."

"No, it didn't," Nick said.

Elizabeth continued. "I don't trust the man who hired us to find it. He's not telling us the whole story. I'm not ready to hand it over to him without finding out what's going on. Something doesn't add up. The sword is worth a lot, but what's been happening is over the top. Too many people have died. Until I know why it's worth piling up bodies, we're keeping it."

"Where is it?" Ronnie asked.

"Here. Well hidden."

"So now you want to talk to this guy in LA to find out why they want it."

"That's right," Nick said.

"Why should he talk to us?" Ronnie asked.

"That's where you come in. We won't get anything out of him without a little intimidation. One look at Lamont, he'll probably tell us what we want to know."

Lamont had an evil looking scar that crossed over his right eye and down the left side of his nose, a hard, pink line caused by shrapnel he'd taken in Iraq.

"Haven't you heard you can't make fun of people these days?" Lamont said. "I ought to turn you over to the PC police."

"Go ahead, but who's going to pay for the pizza later?" Nick said.

"Pepperoni?"

"Whatever you want."

"In that case, I'll forget it. This time."

"Boys," Elizabeth tapped her pen on her desk.

"Sorry, Director," Lamont said.

Selena laughed. "I've missed this."

"The target is a man called Sora Tanaka," Elizabeth said. "He's an under boss, in charge of all yakuza operations on the West Coast. That makes him a big deal. He'll be well protected."

"What's an under boss?" Lamont asked.

"There are four main yakuza families, broken down into more than eight hundred clans. It's a complicated organizational structure, with lots of traditional subcategories that determine rank and status. The only person over Tanaka is the big boss, the man who controls everything in Tanaka's family. He's the Godfather in spades, for real."

"Where does he hang out?"

"Kobe. In Japan."

"At least LA is a lot closer."

"I'm not going to kid you," Elizabeth said. "These people are dangerous. They live by a different set of rules than we do. They make the Mafia look like amateurs. You'll have to find a way to get to Tanaka without going through his soldiers. There have to be times when he's alone, or at least with very few people around him."

"Tell you the truth, I was getting tired of sitting around on my butt waiting for the fish to bite," Lamont said. "I didn't think I'd miss the action, but I do. I'm in."

"Me too," Ronnie said.

"Maybe there won't be any action," Nick said.

"Uh, huh," Lamont said.

TWENTY-ONE

"I've found out a few things about Tanaka, with Freddy's help," Stephanie said. "Being a yakuza boss pays pretty well. He has a three million dollar home in California set on twenty acres."

"Do we know anything about his routines?" Nick asked. "Does he have a regular schedule, predictable patterns?"

"He runs his rackets out of an office in Torrance, right on the main drag. There are several Japanese companies that have their American headquarters in the city. That's resulted in a large Japanese population, second only to Hawaii. Except for occasional trips to Japan, Tanaka is usually in his office during the day. He heads back home in the evening. If you didn't know any better, you'd think he was simply another businessman living in the country and commuting to town for work."

"Yeah, some business," Lamont said. "Drugs, hookers, and extortion. He must be a real nice guy."

"How about nightlife? Does he go to clubs? Bars?" Ronnie asked.

"Sometimes, but not on a regular basis. There's no pattern."

"Is he married? Who's in the house besides him?"

"He was married, but his wife died several years ago in a car accident in Tokyo. The servants live in a separate guest house.

The back of the house. He has a maid, a cook, and a gardener. He calls up an escort service if he wants a woman. There are usually four of his men on the property. One of them acts as a chauffeur. All of them live over the garage. There don't seem to be regular patrols of the grounds."

"He'll have electronic security," Ronnie said.

"Okay," Nick said. "I don't think we should go after him when he's in town. There are too many chances something will go wrong. People could get hurt. That leaves his house. Steph, can you pull up a photo?"

"I thought you might want one. Freddie, please display the satellite shot of Tanaka's house."

Certainly, Stephanie.

A large monitor positioned on a table near Elizabeth's desk lit up with an overhead shot of the house. The building was situated at the end of a long drive. There were no neighbors nearby. A large backyard featured a long swimming pool and broad patio. The yard was bordered with mature trees and backed up to a gentle, grassy slope. The satellite had caught someone on a horse riding along a trail about a hundred yards behind the house.

"Could be worse," Lamont said.

"It could be a lot worse," Nick said. "The house is relatively isolated. We won't have to worry about neighbors, only his guards."

"We can go in from the back," Ronnie said. "Those trees will give us some cover."

"I want to know what kind of alarm systems he's got," Nick said. "Freddie?"

Yes, Nick?

"Can you find out if Tanaka has an alarm service?"

I have already done so. The structure is protected by a national service that operates using cellular connections.

"Remember the good old days when we could cut the phone line?" Ronnie said.

"It's not a problem," Elizabeth said. "We have Hood backing us up, remember? We can jam the cellular signal."

"Sometimes the technology we use to help us out scares the hell out of me," Nick said. "It could come back and bite us some day, if the wrong people get to be in charge of it."

"That's the problem with government, isn't it?" Selena said. "We expect people who run things to respect personal rights and freedom. We expect them to believe in the Constitution. If that ever changes, we'll find ourselves living under a dictatorship before we know what happened. The politicians will spin it to sound like a wonderful thing, but it will be like Nazi Germany or the Soviet Union under Stalin. The only difference is going to be the uniforms of the people with the guns."

"That's a really depressing thought," Stephanie said.

"We're getting off the track," Elizabeth said. "When do you want to do this, Nick?"

"As soon as you set it up with Hood about that alarm system."

"I can do that today."

"We need a private jet. We can't take our weapons on a regular plane."

"That's not a problem. Clarence can have someone meet you with a vehicle when you land."

"Ask him for an SUV. A Suburban, something like that."

"I'm sure it won't be a problem. When do you want to go?"

"If Hood is on board, how about tomorrow? It's the middle of the week. Tanaka probably isn't planning anything special."

There is a first class plane reservation from Los Angeles to Japan in the name of Sora Tanaka, leaving on Friday.

"Then we'd better get our ass in gear," Nick said.

TWENTY-TWO

Sora Tanaka finished showering and walked naked to a wooden hot tub on the other side of the room. The traditional bathroom was one of Tanaka's few indulgences. Wisps of steam rose from the surface of the water circulating through the tub. With a sigh of relief he lowered himself into the water up to his neck, feeling the heat begin its magic. It had been a long day. He hadn't gotten home until late.

Tanaka was angry about Saito's death. As the hot water soothed his body, his anger slowly shifted to reflection. For all his faults, Saito had been a reliable asset, a good soldier. Tanaka found it difficult to understand how the Americans had gotten the best of him, along with Ito and Nakamura. Three seasoned men, members of his clan, his family. Three dead, and he was no closer than before to possessing the sword.

Their deaths would be avenged, but retribution would have to wait until he returned from Japan. It was necessary to travel to Kobe and offer apology to the *oyabun*, Hiro Kobayashi. Tanaka had already made the reservation. He wasn't looking forward to the conversation or the journey, but it was *giri*. Duty.

Perhaps he would lose another piece of a finger, perhaps not. The practice was beginning to fall out of favor with the young, but he and Kobayashi were of an older generation. Whatever happened, he would be expected to have a solution ready. He had failed to carry out his assignment. A deep apology was required.

Saito had picked the home of the Americans as the easier target, and it had gotten him killed. Tanaka believed it more likely that the sword was being kept in their building in Virginia. When he returned from Japan, he would send a larger crew to obtain it. Perhaps he would even lead it himself as part of his redemption. The only potential problem he could see was that Kobayashi might order him to cooperate with the East Coast boss, Watanabe. That would create a problem. Watanabe was a violent and uneducated man. The two men hated each other.

His body now fully relaxed, Tanaka got out of the tub and put on a silk kimono hanging on a hook nearby.

The bathroom was on the ground floor of the house, set off a hall. A pair of sliding glass doors at the end of the hall opened onto the backyard. Moonlight shone from the surface of the pool. Tanaka decided to get a drink and go outside while his body cooled off.

Nick lay in a depression outside the tree line that marked the border of Tanaka's property, watching the house through binoculars. Ronnie and Lamont lay to either side. The moonlight was bright enough that night vision gear wasn't needed. Nick shifted to ease the pressure of the pistol pressing against his leg.

"Someone's come out onto the patio," Ronnie said.

"It's Tanaka," Nick said. "He's wearing some kind of fancy bathrobe."

Tanaka sat down in a chair next to a patio table.

"Going to make it easy for us," Lamont said.

"I don't believe in easy. There has to be a guard somewhere."

Ronnie nudged Nick and pointed at a cluster of trees to the right.

"There. In the trees."

Nick looked through the binoculars. He could make out the dark shape of someone standing in the trees.

"I'll do it," Lamont said.

"Don't kill him," Nick said.

"I'll be real gentle."

Lamont moved away, low against the ground. He disappeared into the trees. Nick kept the binoculars on the guard. A moment later, a dark shape rose up and wrapped an arm around the man's throat. There was a brief struggle. Nick saw Lamont lower the unconscious body to the ground. On the patio, Tanaka showed no sign he'd noticed anything.

Lamont returned, as silently as he'd left.

"He'll be out for a while. I untied him and stuffed a gag in his mouth. He won't be any trouble."

"All right. Let's go talk to Mister Tanaka. Ronnie, you work around to the right. Lamont, you're with me. When we brace him, make sure he can't run for the house. Watch for my signal."

Tanaka was sitting near the pool, a drink resting on the glass top of the patio table. The door back into the house was a good thirty feet away. The area around the patio and the pool was heavily landscaped, with tall plants and flowering bushes. It was a simple matter for Nick and the others to work their way into position. Across the way, Nick saw that Ronnie was in place.

Nick held up three fingers and began counting down.

Three. Two. One.

Tanaka heard the rush of footsteps across the stones of the patio. He turned his head to look and started to rise. Nick reached him and put a pistol against his head.

"Sit down. Now."

Tanaka sat. Lamont pulled his arms behind him and zip tied his wrists together.

"You have made a big mistake," Tanaka said.

"Perhaps. Make sure you don't make one. We only want to talk."

"Do you know who I am?"

"Why do they always say that?" Lamont said. "Of course we know who you are, asshole."

Tanaka looked at him, then at Nick.

"Right now you're wondering why we're here," Nick said. "You sent people to my home. You threatened my children. You're lucky I'm not like you, or you'd be dead now."

"You killed Saito. You're the one who has the sword."

"That's right. Your three thugs are dead. You need to answer my questions, or you're going to join them."

"I'm not afraid of you, or your ugly friend. If you know who I am, then you know I'm not going to tell you anything. You are all dead men."

"Called me ugly. He's beginning to piss me off," Lamont said.

"You can save yourself a lot of trouble," Nick said. "All I want to know is who sent you after the sword, and why. Tell me that, we're gone."

Tanaka remained silent.

"Nick, let's take him inside," Ronnie said.

"You're worried about the noise?"

"Yeah."

"Too much trouble."

Nick took a rag out of his pocket and stuffed it in Tanaka's mouth. For the first time, he saw a trace of concern on Tanaka's face.

"Let me explain something to you," Nick said. "We're not cops. We're not concerned about your well-being. We don't give a shit about the rules. When it comes to people like you, there aren't any rules. We're like you, that way. Except we wouldn't burn down an old people's home to stop someone from talking, or threaten to kill someone's kids to get what we want. As far as I'm concerned, you're a predator who deserves to be shot on sight. So believe me, you're going to tell me what I want to know. Let me demonstrate."

Nick reached down and pinched the nerve center at the base of Tanaka's neck between his thumb and forefinger, hard.

Tanaka writhed in the chair, his scream of pain muffled by the gag. Nick held it for a second then released him. Sweat popped out on Tanaka's forehead as he struggled to recover.

"You understand?"

Tanaka nodded.

"You want to say something?"

Tanaka nodded again.

"Be careful," Nick said. "Don't shout or do anything stupid."

Tanaka nodded. Nick pulled the rag from his mouth.

"You're a dead man," Tanaka sputtered.

"We all die," Nick said. "Don't waste my time. That was only a demonstration. Next time it will last a lot longer and hurt a lot more. Who sent you after the sword?"

"The obayun. He told me to obtain it."

"See, that wasn't so hard. We'd already figured that out. What I want to know is why?"

"I don't know why. I just follow orders."

"Wrong answer."

Nick stuffed the rag back in Tanaka's mouth.

"Ronnie, give me your knife."

"Nick…"

"Don't argue. Give me your damn knife."

Ronnie gave him the knife. It was a type of blade developed by the British in World War II for their commandos. The blade was long and tapered to a sharpened point, razor-sharp on both sides.

Nick lifted up Tanaka's kimono, exposing his genitals. He took the knife and brushed it across the edge of the silk, making a long cut through the material.

"Sharp, isn't it?" Nick said.

He looked down at where Tanaka was exposed.

"Guess what I'm going to do next?"

"Nick, you can't do that," Ronnie said.

"Sure I can. This bastard sent people after my kids. He's forfeited any right to decent treatment."

"Mmmpphhh, mmppphhh," Tanaka said, shaking his head back and forth.

"I think he wants to say something," Lamont said.

Tanaka nodded his head, violently. Nick pulled the gag away.

"Last chance. Why does your boss want the sword?"

"It's political."

"Political?"

"There's a man who wants his candidate to win the next election. We have an alliance with him."

"Nobuyasu?"

"Yes, Nobuyasu. But we don't like his candidate. We want someone else. Nobuyasu will do anything to get the sword.

It gives us leverage over him, control. If we have the sword, Nobuyasu will have to do what we want."

"Why does Nobuyasu want the sword so much that he'll do whatever you say?"

"I don't know. Really, I don't know."

"Hey!"

The shout came from the other end of the yard. Two men had appeared from under the trees. They had pistols.

Nick pressed his pistol into the back of Tanaka's head. "Call them off or you're dead."

Tanaka shouted.

"Sorera o utsu!"

The two men opened fire. Ronnie was struck in the chest and fell backward. Nick fired two shots and brought one of them down. Lamont had his pistol out and fired. Nick felt a burning blow to his head and stumbled. Lamont fired again. The second man screamed and fell.

Tanaka got to his feet and hobbled toward the house, his hands still tied behind the chair.

Lamont shot him, three times. Tanaka stumbled forward and fell onto the flagstones.

"Now who's ugly," Lamont said.

He looked over. Nick swayed on his feet. Blood ran down the side of his face.

"Shit. Nick, you all right?"

Nick pulled a handkerchief from his pocket and held it up against his head to stop the bleeding.

"Yeah. It's only a scalp wound."

Lamont knelt by Ronnie.

Ronnie coughed. "I'm all right. The vest stopped it."

Lamont helped him up.

"Time to boogie," Nick said.

"What about Tanaka?" Lamont said.

Nick walked over to where Tanaka lay on the stones, still bound to the chair. His eyes were open. Blood pooled around him.

"He's done."

"Would you really have cut him?" Ronnie asked.

"No. But he didn't know that."

They disappeared into the night.

TWENTY-THREE

It was no secret that Hiro Kobayashi was head of the most powerful yakuza family in Japan. He controlled a criminal empire that stretched far beyond the borders of his island nation. There was little in the realm of things illegal that didn't interest Kobayashi. Drugs, human trafficking, prostitution, money laundering, loan sharking, gambling – Kobayashi had a hand in all of it. Every human weakness was fair game. Human weakness was an endless, open treasure chest of money for those like Kobayashi who were willing to exploit it.

Kobayashi had started on the lowest rung of the yakuza ladder, back when he was still a boy. Highly intelligent and observant, he had killed his first man before he was twenty. By the time he was thirty, he'd risen all the way to the level of *shateigashira*, a high-ranking lieutenant with many *kyodai* beneath him. It was unusual for a man that young to reach such a high position within the family. He'd been sixty when he was hand-picked by his predecessor to take over the position he now held as boss. That too, was unusual. Most times succession in the family was more a matter of violence than agreement.

At seventy-four years old Kobayashi was a distinctive looking man, every inch the powerful executive. He was of average height, broad shouldered and solid around the waist. His hair was entirely white and cut short. His expensive, dark suit was perfectly tailored and of the best material. The cream-colored shirt he wore gleamed. The knot in his blue silk tie was perfect. From a distance, Kobayashi could easily be mistaken for a wealthy and successful businessman. It was only when you got close and looked into his eyes that you saw something dark and dangerous.

Sometimes, when he was angry, Kobayashi became very still. His eyes would flick back and forth in a way that reminded anyone watching of a poisonous snake waiting to strike. At the moment, he was very angry. He sat at the head of a long table with two men, his eyes darting between his *shingii,* Kensaku Ishimura, and his chief lieutenant, Fumito Izumi. Ishamura was the family's legal advisor, the Japanese equivalent of a mafia *consigliere.*

"Something must be done about these Americans," Kobayashi said. His voice sounded like a shovel scraping across gravel, the result of a blow to the throat he taken years before. The man who'd struck him had died a few seconds later.

When he was sure Kobayashi was finished speaking, Fumito Izumi spoke.

"We have been humiliated by Tanaka's death and his failure to obtain the sword. The other families have learned of it and see it as a sign we are becoming weak. We must retaliate. It is not acceptable."

"I advise caution," Ishimura said. "These particular Americans are well connected with their CIA. Of course we must avenge this dishonor, but we cannot risk a direct confrontation with the American government."

"You always advise caution. You are like an old woman with her basket of fish. There's a time for caution and a time for action. This is one of those times."

"Deru kui wa utareru," Ishimura said. "The stake that sticks up will be hammered down."

"There are many proverbs," Izumi said. "I prefer the one that tells us fear is greater than danger. Taking out these people who have stained our honor will be easier than you expect."

"You are both forgetting what is important," Kobayashi said. "The sword. Nobuyasu is obsessed with it. With the sword, we control Nobuyasu. With Nobuyasu, we control the future of our nation. The sword can bring us power that has not been seen since the days of the shogunate."

Izumi said, "With your permission, boss, let me send Watanabe after the sword. He's already in America. He could do it."

"You'd send Watanabe?" Ishimura said. "He's a loose cannon. He'll attract too much attention."

"The other families need to know they can't screw around with us. Watanabe will paint the walls with blood. We need to send a clear message. Word will get around. Our reputation will be restored."

"And the CIA?"

"Fuck the CIA. What can they do? They know who we are, they know what we do, and they profit from it. They don't want to rock the boat. A few dead Americans? They're not going to come after us over something like that."

Kobayashi held up his hand. "Enough."

Izumi and Ishimura looked at him and waited for his decision.

"Fujito, you have my permission to contact Watanabe. Give him the information he needs. Tell him this is a priority assignment. Tell him that success brings reward."

"Boss..." Ishimura said.

Kobayashi looked at him. Ishimura had been at Kobayashi's side for many years and recognized the look. It sent a chill down his spine.

"I have made my decision," Kobayashi said.

"Yes, boss."

"Good."

Ishimura thought he would not like to be in the Americans' shoes when Watanabe came calling.

TWENTY-FOUR

Nick and the others were back in Virginia. The bullet fired at Nick had grazed the side of his head. A centimeter to the right, he'd be dead.

"It would have been better if no one had gotten killed," Elizabeth said.

"We didn't have a choice," Nick said. "He'd told us what we needed to know. I was almost done. Then his goons came out of the woods and started shooting."

"There's bound to be fallout from this," Selena said.

"What kind of fallout? The cops don't know we were there."

"I'm not talking about the cops. I'm talking about the yakuza. By killing one of their principal bosses, you've started a war with them. They'll figure out who it was. When they do, their honor will demand revenge. They're going to come after us."

"They already tried that and it didn't work."

"They didn't expect a big problem before. It will be different next time."

"You're a real optimist," Ronnie said.

"Everything I know about Japanese culture tells me it's only a question of time before they send a hit squad. They won't mess around. It will be more than a few people, and they'll all be well armed. They have to kill us to avenge Tanaka and the insult to their honor."

"What a bunch of crap," Lamont said. "Gangsters with honor."

"Say what you like, but they take the concept of honor seriously. The code they live by doesn't give them an option. They must come after us. And don't forget that we still have the sword."

"I wish I'd never heard of Masamune," Elizabeth said. "Now we know why the yakuza want it, but we still don't know why Nobuyasu thinks it's so important."

"Tanaka seemed certain possession of the sword would give his boss control over Nobuyasu. Control of Nobuyasu means control of the next election."

"Is Nobuyasu really that powerful?" Stephanie asked.

"He's one of the richest men in Japan," Elizabeth said. "Yes, he's really that powerful. It's more than money, he has a samurai bloodline and he's well known to the public. He's been very careful to cultivate a public image of service to the country and its traditional values. He was one of the first to publicly praise the new Emperor and vow allegiance to the chrysanthemum throne."

"But the Emperor doesn't have any real power," Stephanie said.

"No, but as a national symbol and head of the Shinto religion, he's extremely important. The Constitution created after the war stripped him of his assumed divine origin, but many people still revere him as a descendent of the sun goddess. Especially the older generations."

"They believe this stuff?" Ronnie said.

"Japan is a complicated place," Selena said. "It's not a good idea to judge it from a Western point of view."

"Okay, I get it," Nick said. "Nobuyasu is a big deal."

"I've been doing a little digging into Nobuyasu," Stephanie said. "All is not quite what it appears to be with our Japanese industrialist."

"What do you mean?" Elizabeth asked.

"You said earlier that he was one of the wealthiest men in Japan. That's true on paper, but he's got serious financial problems. He's on the edge of going bankrupt. He invested heavily in an ocean seabed mining venture that went belly up and made some other high-risk investments that aren't doing well. He also likes to visit Macau and do a little gambling, where he's considered a high roller. Put it all together, and he's in trouble."

"Maybe that's why he wants the sword," Ronnie said. "It has to be worth millions. He could sell it on the black market."

"That wouldn't bring enough to make up for his losses," Stephanie said. "But if he and his Black Swan Society can put their man in office, he stands to benefit from government contracts. He needs those contracts to survive."

"And now his buddies in the yakuza have decided they want someone else. I wouldn't want to be in his shoes," Nick said.

Elizabeth tapped her pen on her desk.

"We're getting off the subject. Selena, you're sure these people will come after us for revenge?"

"Yes. I'm certain they will."

"Then we need to plan for it."

"That presents some problems," Nick said. "We don't know when they'll make their move or where. It's hard to plan for something like that."

"We need to make some assumptions," Selena said. "That usually gives us a handle on the best course of action."

"Okay," Stephanie said. "What's our first assumption?"

"That's easy. A bunch of wannabe samurai are pissed at us and want to take us off the board," Lamont said.

"That's one way to put it," Selena said. "Then assumption number one is that the yakuza want to kill us."

"Assumption number two?" Nick asked.

"They want the sword. So before they kill everyone, they have to find out where it's hidden," Ronnie said.

"That works," Lamont said. "What's assumption number three?"

"Freddie, are you keeping a record of this?" Stephanie said.

Yes, Stephanie. This is quite interesting. May I contribute to the discussion?

They looked at each other. This was something new.

"Sure, Freddie," Stephanie said.

Nick, you said it was hard to plan something when you don't know when or where they'll make their move.

"That's right."

The solution to that problem seems simple.

They waited. The computer was silent.

Stephanie sighed. "Freddie, please tell us your solution."

If you make the enemy think you will be in a specific place at a specific time and in possession of the sword, you will know where and when they will attack. Then you will be prepared to defeat them.

"A trap," Nick said.

That is correct.

"You know, that could work," Ronnie said.

"Pretty sneaky for a bunch of electronic circuits," Lamont said.

"Careful, you'll hurt his feelings," Stephanie said. "You should apologize."

"Freddie is a computer."

"He has feelings, Lamont."

"Sorry, Freddie. I didn't mean anything."

Your apology is accepted.

"See what I mean?"

"Then assumption number three is we set a trap to draw these people to us, so we can eliminate the threat?" Nick said.

"I like it," Ronnie said. "It gives us the initiative, instead of sitting around waiting for the bad guys to start something."

"Me too," Lamont said.

"We're talking about a full out war. You realize that, don't you?" Selena said.

"Do you have a better idea?" Nick said.

"I thought we were done with all of this. You were almost killed yesterday. Now we're talking about laying an ambush for a bunch of hard-core criminals who think they have a debt of honor that has to be paid. Don't you see what's wrong with this picture?"

"There's a lot wrong with it. I get it, and I don't like it, but we don't have any choice. If they're coming after us, we have to take them out first. Whatever it takes."

"Why don't we give the sword to Nobuyasu and be done with it? Once they know we don't have it, they may leave us alone."

"You really believe that?"

"They want this sword more than anything else. If we give it to Nobuyasu, it changes the dynamic. The sword is their priority, not us."

"You just got through telling us they have to get even for Tanaka. That it's a debt of honor and they have to come after us."

"That's true. But I don't want them coming after us here. It's too risky. What are we going to do, turn this building into a fortress? You know that's not going to work."

"She's got a point, Nick," Ronnie said. "Our old HQ was hardened, but this place will be tough to defend."

"We can't stay together all the time," Selena said. "All they have to do is wait and pick us off one by one."

Elizabeth tapped her pen. "I have to say something. First off, I'd like to remind all of you that we no longer have presidential protection. It's not like before. It won't go over well if we get in a pitched gun battle with a bunch of yakuza thugs."

"What about our relationship with Langley?" Nick asked. "I thought we had some protection."

"DCI Hood is willing to help us out, but there's a limit. If we get in a shoot out on American soil, he can't protect us. It would be a mess. The way things are now, we'd probably be accused of hate crimes because the yakuza are Japanese. It wouldn't matter that they started it or had tried to kill us. But he can help in other ways. Selena, are you suggesting we take the sword to Nobuyasu?"

"That's exactly what I'm suggesting."

"He's in Japan," Elizabeth said.

"Then we take the sword to Japan. That's where it belongs, anyway."

Elizabeth picked up her pen and set it down again, thinking. They waited for her to speak.

"Hood knows the man who heads up Japan's version of the CIA, Daichi Yamamoto. He told me Yamamoto thinks Nobuyasu and his Black Swan group are a threat to Japan's democracy. He wants to find a way to take them down. Freddie's idea of setting a trap is a good one. What if we could do it over there, with official support? I'm sure Yamamoto wouldn't want the yakuza to get their hands on that sword."

"That might work."

"I'll call Clarence and see what he can do."

TWENTY-FIVE

Daichi Yamamoto considered the latest intelligence concerning China. There was always something in the daily brief about China. Recent angry pronouncements from Beijing regarding Taiwan and supposed Chinese sovereignty over the Straits of Taiwan were a cause of deep concern. Fully ninety percent of the container traffic and shipping that was the lifeblood of Japan moved through those waters. If the PRC ever decided to block the waterway, it would create a crisis that could easily trigger world war.

Yamamoto looked up in annoyance as his intercom buzzed. He'd left specific orders not to be disturbed.

"Yes."

"Sir, CIA director Hood is holding on line two."

Hood. What did he want? Perhaps it was something about the sword. Yamamoto picked up his phone.

"Clarence. To what do I owe the pleasure?"

Yamamoto's English was excellent.

"There have been some developments here, Daichi. Have you got a few minutes?"

"Of course, my friend. I always have time for you."

"I'm sure you've been thinking about the latest threats coming out of Beijing, but that isn't why I'm calling. It's about the Masamune sword."

"Ah."

"We have recovered it. Two people I trust with my life are going to bring it to you. But it's complicated, and I would like your help. Please allow me to explain."

Hood told Yamamoto about events in the United States, how the sword had been found and that the yakuza were now involved. He told him about Tanaka.

"Tanaka is dead?"

"As yesterday's fish."

"He was an important man in the yakuza organization," Yamamoto said. "The obayun is a man called Kobayashi. I know him. He will not let this pass without retaliation."

"That is one of the reasons I'm calling. I am hoping you can use your considerable influence to prevent this from escalating. Before he died, Tanaka revealed that the yakuza no longer support Nobuyasu's choice for premier in the next election. Nobuyasu's obsession with the sword makes it the perfect tool to pressure him, and through him the keiretsu. Kobayashi wants his man to lead your country."

So that was the game the yakuza were playing!

"You are giving me a headache," Yamamoto said, "but what you are telling me explains some things happening here."

Hood laughed. Then he laid out the idea that a trap might be set in Japan for Nobuyasu, using the sword as bait.

"I know you'd like to get something on Nobuyasu. Are you aware of his financial situation?"

"We are. It is something of a problem. The collapse of his financial empire would shake our economy. It is like what you say about your banks. What is it? Too big to fail?"

"That's right. I'm afraid I can't help you with that, but I assume that if you had leverage over Nobuyasu it would be helpful."

"It could be."

"Am I correct in assuming that as a declared national treasure, the Honjo Masamune belongs in the custody of the government?"

"That is correct."

"Then if Nobuyasu takes possession of the sword and fails to inform the government, he has committed a crime."

"That is also correct. I see where you are going, Clarence."

"We are convinced Nobuyasu has an ulterior motive for obtaining the sword. We don't know what it is, but I'm certain it would be of interest to you. The yakuza are a serious threat to my friends. You know of them as the Project. They currently have possession of the sword."

"Ah."

"They are more than friends. My agency has an unofficial relationship with them. The threat the yakuza represent is something I can't ignore. Do you think you can get them to back off?"

"It would be difficult," Yamamoto said. "The yakuza have a traditional interpretation of honor and revenge. The death of someone as important as Tanaka will be seen as a direct stain on their honor. The other families will be watching to see what Kobayashi does. He's getting old, and there are elements within his family that want a change in leadership. He must not display anything that can be interpreted as weakness. I do not think I can convince him to forgo vengeance."

"I was afraid you'd say that," Hood said. "You understand my concern."

"You are right to be concerned, but even Kobayashi will hesitate to provoke my agency. I can offer protection while your people are here. He would be foolish to try something."

"I would like them to be armed," Hood said. "In case something happens."

"I'm afraid that will not be possible," Yamamoto said. "We have very strict rules about guns here. However, my agents will be armed. I'm sure your friends will be safe."

"I understand. I appreciate your help."

"Tell me the names of the people who will bring the sword."

"Nick Carter and Selena Connor. Selena speaks fluent Japanese."

"That will be most helpful."

"When I have the details of their flight, I'll let you know. I expect it will be in a day or two."

"Excellent. I will have them met at the airport."

"Thank you for your assistance, Yamamoto-san. I wish you luck with Nobuyasu."

The two men shared a few pleasantries and ended the conversation.

Yamamoto put down his phone and thought about what he'd just learned. His mind turned over the possibilities.

Nobuyasu was in possession of highly embarrassing photographs that would destroy Yamamoto's career if they were ever made public. Dismissal from government service would only be the beginning of his problems. The humiliation would be unbearable.

For some reason Nobuyasu was obsessed with the Honjo Masamune. The return of the sword to Japan might provide an opportunity to force him to hand over the incriminating photographs and negatives. As head of the PSIA, Yamamoto had many tools at his disposal. Such a shame, if an important man like Nobuyasu were to meet with an unfortunate accident while attempting to illegally appropriate a national treasure. Perhaps an opportunity would present itself after the Americans arrived.

It was a happy thought.

TWENTY-SIX

It was raining when Nick and Selena arrived at Narita International Airport. As usual, Selena had upgraded their seats to first class, a real luxury on the long flight. As soon as the door on the plane opened, two men in dark business suits came in. They went directly to where Nick and Selena were seated.

"You are Nicholas Carter and Doctor Connor?" one of the men said.

"That's right."

"Welcome to Japan. I am Kensaku. This is my partner, Akio. We've been sent to escort you to your hotel. Everything has been arranged. Please."

"You are from the Public Security Agency, Kensaku-san?" Selena asked in perfect Japanese.

Kensaku managed to conceal his surprise.

"That is correct." He replied in the same language.

"May I see your identification?" she said.

Kensaku showed his credentials. He gestured at the open door.

"Please."

Everyone in the cabin was watching, wondering if the two Americans were being arrested. Nick and Selena got out of their seats. Nick took down their bags from the overhead bin, then the package containing the Masamune sword. Carrying the lethal weapon onto the plane had been arranged by DCI Hood. It was inside a titanium case with biometric lock only Nick or Selena could open.

They followed the escort out of the plane, down the walkway, and into the airport. They went through a side door and bypassed the line at passport control.

"May I have your passports?" Kensaku said.

They handed them over. Kensaku gave the documents to a customs official. He gave them a cursory look and stamped them. Kensaku gave them back to Nick. They walked down a long passage and emerged onto the main floor of the terminal. A gray Nissan waited for them outside.

The area was crowded with hundreds of people. They put the bags into the trunk. Nick kept the sword with him. No one noticed a man watching Nick and Selena climb into the car, or noticed when he spoke into what looked like a Bluetooth earpiece.

Nick and Selena sat in the back of the car, the two escorts in the front. Kensaku turned around so he could face them.

"We're about sixty kilometers from the city. Traffic can be difficult. The drive will take about an hour, perhaps more. This rain may slow us up."

"Are you taking us to our hotel?" Selena asked.

"Yes. Director Yamamoto thought you would like to refresh yourselves and relax a bit after your long flight. He invites you to have dinner with him at seven this evening. He prefers someplace a bit more private than the restaurants in your hotel. Akio and I will take you there, and you can give him the sword at that time. Until then we will remain outside your room as a precaution."

"A precaution?" Nick said.

"A courtesy, really. We do not expect anything unusual to happen."

"Good. I'm a little tired of unusual."

Traffic was heavy. They reached a junction where the road from the airport joined the E51 and turned left toward Tokyo. The traffic reminded Nick of an evening in Los Angeles, bumper-to-bumper and moving slowly, sometimes starting and stopping. Rain pattered on the roof of the car, glistening on the dark pavement.

"This is worse than usual," Kensaku said. "There must be an accident."

They crept along. After several minutes they came upon the cause of the delay. A white minivan and a blue car had collided, blocking one of the lanes. Bits of glass and metal were strewn across the road. A motorcycle cop directed traffic around the wreckage. As their car reached the accident, the cop held up his hand to stop them.

"What now?" Kensaku said.

Akio was driving. He rolled down his window as the cop came up to the car.

Nick's ear began itching.

"Something's wrong," he said.

The motorcycle cop reached the car, took out a gun, and shot Akio in the head. Blood spattered over the windshield, misting across the inside of the car. His second shot hit Kensaku as he reached for the gun under his jacket. Two men jumped out of the white van and ran to the car. They had guns. One of them pulled open the passenger door.

Nick slammed the case with the sword into the man's face. Stunned, the attacker fell backward, dropping his gun. Nick rolled out of the car, grabbed the gun, and fired at the second man, bringing him down. The first man was struggling to his feet. Nick shot him, then turned. The phony cop had his pistol pointed at Selena's head. He shouted something in Japanese.

"Nick, he'll kill me. He says drop the gun. He wants the sword. Give it to him. He means it."

Nick stood in the rain, the lights of a thousand commuter cars lighting up the wet pavement. The cop pressed his gun against Selena's head. His face was contorted, angry.

Ready to pull the trigger.

"Okay, I'm dropping the gun." Nick dropped the pistol on the ground and raised his hands. "Tell him he can have the sword."

Selena let off a stream of Japanese. The man said something back.

"He says take the sword to the motorcycle and strap it on the back. He says hurry or he shoots."

"All right."

Nick picked up the case with the sword and went to the motorcycle. Bungee cords were wrapped around a carrier on the back of the bike. He used the cords to strap the sword to the carrier and stepped away.

Still holding the gun on Selena, the man barked out a command and began moving away from the car, toward the bike.

"He says back away or he'll shoot."

Nick took several steps back. The man pushed Selena away and shifted his aim to Nick. He went to the bike, straddled it, and kicked away the stand, his gun trained on Nick the whole time. The bike was a Honda VFR, big, fast, and powerful. He punched the ignition button. It fired up instantly. With a practiced motion, the man stuffed the gun in his jacket, grabbed the handle bars and took off. By the time Nick could react, the machine and the sword were already a hundred feet away. He watched the taillight disappear into the rain filled night.

Selena got out of the car.

"Are you all right?" he said.

"I'm fine. Just annoyed with myself."

"Why?"

"There was one point when I might've been able to disarm him."

"Sure, or get yourself killed. I'm going to check Kensaku."

There wasn't any point in checking Akio. Most of his brains were scattered around the inside of the car. Nick opened the door and felt Kensaku's neck for a pulse.

"He's still alive."

Selena had a phone in her hand. "I'm on it."

Minutes later sirens sounded in the distance.

TWENTY-SEVEN

Yamamoto was not a happy man. Word had leaked that the sword had returned to Japan and been stolen. It was a disaster, both personally and professionally. In Japan, there was little room for the avoidance of responsibility. Yamamoto knew the future of his career was at stake. If he failed to recover the sword within a reasonable time, he would be replaced. His past successes would be forgotten, his name stained with the shame of failure. He would be forever known as the man who had allowed the Honjo Masamune to fall into the hands of criminals.

It was unfair, but it was the way things were.

Nick and Selena had been brought to public security headquarters in Chiyoda City, a special ward within Tokyo. They'd been offered tea and placed in a room with Western-style furniture that was comfortable enough. A man stood guard outside the door. They weren't prisoners, but it was clear they were not free to go.

"How did the bad guys know we were coming to Japan?" Nick said. "It wasn't public knowledge."

"They must have been watching us," Selena said. "It would be simple enough. Follow us to the airport, find out what flight we were on, and go on from there."

"These people are really well-organized. Setting up a professional ambush like that? I have to hand it to them."

"You surprised that first man, hitting him with the sword case like that."

"He's lucky it wasn't the sword."

The door opened. Daichi Yamamoto entered, accompanied by a personal assistant carrying a laptop. Nick and Selena stood.

"Mister Carter, Doctor Connor. I am Daichi Yamamoto. I'm sorry for the inconvenient delay. I hope you haven't had an unpleasant wait?"

"The tea was excellent," Selena said.

"Please, sit."

They sat. Yamamoto said to Nick, "I understand you disabled two of the attackers. That was well done."

The assistant began recording the interview.

"Thanks. Tell me, how is your agent, Kensaku?"

"I am sorry to say that he died an hour ago."

"Shit."

"Yes. That is an appropriate comment. Still, you did what you could."

"I wish I could have prevented the loss of the sword. The third man would have killed Selena. There wasn't anything I could do."

"What did you notice about this third man?"

"He was a little shorter than you, and his face was rounder. He looked like one of your policemen. His bike looked like a police bike. He had a police helmet on and a radio clipped to his shoulder. They had it set up to look like an accident. Akio never had a chance. The man signaled us to stop. As soon as Akio rolled down his window, he shot him, then he shot Kensaku."

"And then?"

"Then two men with guns piled out of the white van and ran toward us. I opened the door and hit the first one with the sword case. I picked up his gun and shot the second man. That was when Selena told me to stop or the phony cop would kill her."

"You are convinced he meant to shoot?"

"I was. His face was distorted with anger. He looked like one of your old samurai prints, except he had a gun instead of a sword. I knew he'd kill her if I didn't do what he said."

"What happened next?"

"He told me to strap the case with the sword onto the bike. Then he switched his aim over to me and told me to step away. I did. He got on the bike and took off."

"The case was locked, *neh*?"

"Yes, with biometrics. It's made out of titanium. Someone can cut into it."

"How do you think they knew you were coming here with the sword?"

"We were just talking about that," Selena said. "We think we were followed to the airport."

"You saw no one at the time?"

"No," Nick said.

"Very well," Yamamoto said. "This is now out of your hands. It's strictly our business now."

"We would like to help," Selena said.

"You can help by sitting down with one of our sketch artists and helping him make a picture of the man who took the sword."

"We can do more than that," Nick said.

"Thank you for your offer, but you are foreigners here. Aside from the sketch, there's nothing more you can do. I would like you to stay in Japan for now, in case I need to talk to you again. We will be responsible for your hotel bill. Please enjoy your stay."

Yamamoto stood. Nick and Selena got up. Yamamoto bowed.

"Please accept my sincere apologies for the inconvenience to you and the criminal actions of my countrymen."

Selena and Nick bowed. Selena said something in Japanese and bowed.

Yamamoto bowed again and left the room.

"What did you say?" Nick asked.

"I thanked him and told him we accepted his sincere apology and appreciated his courtesy."

"I think I'm beginning to get the hang of this bowing thing," Nick said.

TWENTY-EIGHT

Anyone who happened to be outside the hotel when Hiro Kobayashi arrived with his entourage would have been able to tell from the deep, full bows of the hotel staff that this was an important man. Everyone knew who Kobayashi was. For many Japanese he was a kind of folk hero, a man who had found a way to honor the rigid traditions of Japanese culture while at the same time breaking free of them. In Japan, that was no easy thing to accomplish.

Several limousines lined the drive in front of the hotel. Kobayashi was the last to arrive at the meeting. The manager of the hotel bowed low as he came through the doors.

"Kobayashi-san, welcome. Please allow me to escort you to the others."

Kobayashi acknowledged the man with a slight bow and followed him down a corridor to the conference room. The center of the room was taken up by a large, rectangular table. A half dozen comfortable chairs were placed around the table. Five of the chairs were occupied. Kobayashi took the empty seat at the head.

Three of the men sitting at the table were obayun in their own right, the bosses of the other three major yakuza crime families. The fourth and fifth chairs were taken up by Atagi Nobuyasu and one of his

brothers from the Black Swan Society,
another member of the keiretsu.

Kobayashi was pleased to see that
Nobuyasu was struggling to conceal his
anger and frustration. Emotion clouded
judgment. It was always good when the
inner harmony of one's opponent was
disturbed.

Several men stood away from the table
against the walls, behind their respective
bosses. Each had proved his loyalty and
fearlessness. Each wore a dark suit, white
shirt, and tie. They stood with their hands
clasped in front of them, silent and
unsmiling, their guns hidden under tailored
jackets.

The tension in the room was like the
heavy feel of weighted air that comes before
a storm.

"Let us begin," Kobayashi said.

Nobuyasu said, "Millions have been
wasted preparing for the election of our
candidate. Yet now you have chosen
someone else. I thought you were an
honorable man."

"Be careful what you say, Nobuyasu."

Kobayashi's voice was quiet, but no one
doubted the threat hidden within it.

"I will say what is true. Why have you
reneged on our agreement?"

In a room above the conference table
where the men sat, two of Yamamoto's
agents sat listening to the conversation. A
recorder was capturing every word.

"We discovered certain, ah,
vulnerabilities to the man you and your

friends had picked. Were you aware of his proclivity for young children?"

Nobuyasu tried to hide his surprise, not very successfully.

"No? I thought not. It would have come out during the campaign, sooner or later."

"I do not believe what you are saying," Nobuyasu said. "We thoroughly vetted him."

Kobayashi snapped his fingers. One of the men standing behind him reached under his jacket. Everyone watched. His hand came out with an envelope. He walked over to where Nobuyasu sat and placed it in front of him, then returned to his spot by the wall.

"The pictures in that envelope will convince you," Kobayashi said. "You and your society will support our candidate. This is not open for discussion."

The other yakuza chiefs nodded.

"You see?" Kobayashi said. "We are all in agreement. We have discussed this at length."

"And if we don't support your man?"

"That would be unfortunate. But things don't have to become unpleasant. I have something to exchange for your cooperation."

"You have nothing I want," Nobuyasu said.

"Not even the Honjo Masamune?"

Nobuyasu stiffened.

"You have the sword? Why should I believe you?"

In answer, Kobayashi took out an envelope and slid it across the table to Nobuyasu.

Nobuyasu looked at Kobayashi, tore open the envelope, and looked at the picture inside. It showed the sword, next to a Tokyo newspaper with the day's date. There was no mistaking it for anything else. At the sight of the one thing he most desired in the world, Nobuyasu's heart began beating hard in his chest.

The sword!

He looked at Kobayashi across the table and thought about killing him.

"Do not make a mistake," Kobayashi said. "If you try to do what you are thinking, you will die. Here. Today."

Nobuyasu made an effort to control his emotions. This was not the time.

"I must consult with the others," Nobuyasu said.

"Of course," Kobayashi said. "Remember. This is not negotiable."

He rose. The other obayun rose with him. Nobuyasu and his companion remained seated as the four yakuza and their guards left the room.

"Kobayashi is a snake," Nobuyasu's companion said. "I suspected he couldn't be trusted."

"We must talk with the others and decide how to respond."

"He and his people can make a lot of trouble for us."

"What he fails to remember is that we can make a lot of trouble for him. He and his criminal friends have gone too far this time. We will have to do something about them."

In the room above, Yamamoto's men looked at each other.

"Wait till the director hears this," one of them said.

TWENTY-NINE

Nick and Selena were having breakfast in the hotel. Selena was reading a Japanese newspaper.

"There's a special exhibition of Muramasa swords at the Tokyo National Museum this week," she said. "I'd like to see that."

"Who was Muramasa?"

"He was another famous sword smith. Unlike Masamune, his swords aren't considered national treasures. But they are extremely well known and very popular in pop culture. There's even a video game built around a Muramasa sword."

"There seems to be a national obsession with these weapons."

"I suppose you could say that. Japan's feudal past makes our Wild West look like Sesame Street. There are lots of famous samurai, and all of them had swords. Muramasa's swords are considered cursed. That makes them even more interesting."

"Cursed? Why?"

"Many famous samurai died because of them. There's a myth that when one of Muramasa's swords is drawn, it has to taste blood before it can be put back in the scabbard. If it has to, it will turn on its owner to draw blood. A lot of people take the story seriously."

"Great. Demon swords. And you want to go look at them?"

"It will be fun," Selena said.

The Tokyo National Museum was one of the great art museums in the world. It consisted of five separate buildings located in a sprawling park in the middle of Tokyo. The swords were being displayed in the *Honkan* building, which was dedicated solely to Japanese art. The National Treasure Gallery was in the Honkan building.

They got to the museum shortly after it had opened for the day. It was not yet crowded by Japanese standards, but there were still hundreds of people milling about the exhibition halls. The Muramasa swords were being displayed on the second floor. There were perhaps a dozen swords being exhibited.

"Muramasa made a lot of swords," Selena said. "His blades have a distinctive style to them."

They paused in front of a glass cabinet. The Muramasa sword rested on a rack draped with a piece of gray silk. The cutting-edge was turned upward. The ancient steel gleamed under the light. A shadowy, wavelike pattern danced along the edge, forged within the steel.

"That is one nasty looking weapon," Nick said.

"As a work of art, it's beautiful," Selena said. "Look at the curve. Look at the proportions. I'll bet that blade is as sharp as the day it was finished."

As he looked at the sword, Nick saw a reflection in the glass. A man was coming up behind them. Something about the way he moved toward them set off warning bells. In the glass, Nick saw him reach inside his jacket and draw a pistol.

"Down!"

He pushed Selena as the gun fired. The glass cabinet shattered. An alarm started blaring. People began screaming.

Something made Selena reach into the cabinet and take the Muramasa sword from the rack. She gripped the hilt in two hands and turned toward the attacker. He fired again and missed. She closed on him with a guttural cry and brought the sword down in a sweeping arc. It sliced through his shoulder, then down through his chest and abdomen, as if cutting through butter.

Blood sprayed across the room. Selena pulled the sword out. The man stood for a second, unsure what had happened. The sword had cleaved his arm and shoulder from his body and opened up his chest. Selena could see daylight through the wound.

He toppled to the floor.

"Holy shit," Nick said.

Selena looked down at the sword in her hand. Blood dripped from the blade. She looked up at Nick.

"What have I done?" she said.

THIRTY

They were arrested and separated. Nine and a half hours later they were released into the custody of the Public Security Intelligence Agency.

Once again they found themselves in a room at the agency headquarters with a guard at the door.

"What made you grab the sword?" Nick asked.

"I don't know," she said. "It was almost as if something took over my body. Everything went into slow motion. You know what that's like."

Nick nodded. It happened sometimes in combat.

"I knew I had to pick up the sword. When I did, it felt like an electric current went through my body."

"You're kidding."

"No. It was the strangest thing I've ever felt, as if the sword took over. I mean, I know what to do, I've practiced sword forms for years. But this was different."

"You were so fast," Nick said. "I've never seen anything like it. When you struck, the sword was a blur."

"It makes me wonder if there's some truth in that old myth about the Muramasa swords being evil."

"You think that sword is possessed? Come on, Selena."

"I don't know if it's possessed or not. But you weren't the one who was holding it."

"I wonder who that guy was. Who sent him after us."

The door opened as Nick was speaking. Yamamoto entered.

"He was yakuza. They have a grudge against you."

They started to rise. Yamamoto gestured for them to stay sitting and took a chair across from them.

"Doctor Connor, you are now a cult hero. Don't be surprised if you find yourself depicted as a character in the next version of the video games that feature Muramasa swords."

"I don't feel like a hero," Selena said.

"The press has gone insane with this."

Yamamoto handed her a paper. The front-page had a large photograph of Selena as she was about to strike the gunman. Her face was contorted with fury. Muramasa's sword was a silver streak in the air.

"Oh, my," she said.

"Damn phones," Nick said. "Everybody's a photographer."

"Do you know the stories about the Muramasa blades?"

"I do. We were just talking about it."

The room was bugged. Yamamoto already knew what had been said. He decided there was no need to tell them that.

"What you did today added to the legends. The fact that you are a foreigner and a woman makes it even more extraordinary."

"You said the yakuza have a grudge against us," Nick said. "Why do you think that?"

"The yakuza don't attack people at random. Most likely it is payback for Tanaka."

"We knew they might come after us, but Tanaka called the shots. I didn't kill him on purpose."

"That doesn't matter. It's a matter of honor for the yakuza, particularly for Hiro Kobayashi. Tanaka worked under him. You have a powerful enemy."

"I think it's time for us to go home," Nick said. "If this guy is as powerful as you say, we'd be better off on our home turf."

"It doesn't matter where you are if Kobayashi wants you dead," Yamamoto said.

"You're a real bundle of joy, Yamamoto-san," Nick said.

Selena looked at Yamamoto.

"You sound as though you have something in mind."

"As a matter of fact, I do," he said.

THIRTY-ONE

It was two thirty in the morning in Virginia. Everyone except Stephanie was asleep. After Nick and Selena left for Japan, Elizabeth called a meeting. They decided that until the yakuza threat was resolved, everyone would stay at the house in Virginia. Elizabeth wanted Stephanie to go home, out of the line of fire, but she refused.

"Lucas can look after Matthew while I'm here," she said.

"Are you sure? If someone comes after us, it could get nasty."

"I'm sure."

"We could be here for a while."

"I'm staying."

No more was said about it.

There was plenty of room in the house. They had weapons, a well-stocked kitchen, the pool table, and exercise machines. It wasn't exactly roughing it.

Elizabeth, Ronnie, and Lamont all had rooms on the second floor. So did Stephanie, but she'd been unable to sleep. She was in the ground-floor library, working with her laptop on an enhancement for Freddie.

Security at the new headquarters wasn't as extensive as it had been at the old Project HQ, but there were motion sensors outside and silent alarms triggered by a laser grid. It wasn't possible to approach the building without detection when the alarm system was active. Installing security features had been at the top of Elizabeth's list when she took over the building.

Stephanie was absorbed in her task and didn't notice the red light flashing in back of her.

Stephanie, there are intruders.

She looked up and saw the light.

"Freddie, wake the others. Make sure everything is locked."

Yes, Stephanie.

"Call the cops. Whoever it is means us harm. Do whatever you can to help."

Yes, Stephanie.

Stephanie reached into the drawer of the desk and took out her pistol. She turned off the light on the desk and ran to the front of the building and up the stairs.

Ronnie and Lamont were already up and in the hall outside of their rooms. Lamont was barefoot. Two spare magazines were tucked in the waistband of his shorts. Ronnie had pulled on a pair of pants. He, too, had his pistol in hand. Elizabeth came out into the hall, dressed in a nightgown and holding a pistol. Moonlight came through the big glass dome over the atrium, casting a pale glow over the stairs and floor below.

"We've got visitors," Stephanie said.

Downstairs, they heard glass break.

Ronnie said, "They're in the house. Director, you and Stephanie head up to the next floor. If we have to retreat, you cover us. Lamont, we'll wait on the balcony. We've got the high ground. They have to come up the stairs."

Below, they heard muffled words.

"Director. Go."

Elizabeth and Stephanie hurried up to the third floor.

The stairs from below rose in a curve on the right of the atrium to a long balcony that looked down on the floor below. Stairs to the third story began at the left end of the balcony. Lamont stood on the right end of the balcony, out of sight from the floor below. He could see down into the atrium and the entrance to the room with the pool table. Ronnie moved to the other end, where he had a full view of the stairs coming up from below and the door into the library.

They waited.

Two men dressed in black outfits emerged from the back of the house, then a third. They were holding machine pistols. From where he stood, Lamont thought they looked like Uzis. He held up three fingers to Ronnie across the way.

Ronnie nodded.

Freddie's electronic voice boomed out through the house.

You have entered a secured area. Police have been called. Leave now.

The three men froze. A fourth man appeared, also carrying an Uzi. It was a lot more firepower than Ronnie and Lamont could muster with their two pistols.

The men moved out of Lamont's view and started up the stairs. Ronnie waited until they were halfway, then opened up. Lamont stepped out and fired until the slide locked back on his pistol. One of the intruders got off a burst before he went down. The bullets stitched a pattern across the wall and tore into the painting of Washington.

Three more men appeared, blasting away, filling the space along the balcony with flying bits of plaster and white dust. Someone shouted in Japanese.

Lamont ducked back, ejected, and slammed in a fresh magazine. He waited for a pause in the shooting, then ran across the balcony, firing as he went. He made it across to where Ronnie was firing down into the atrium. Screams came from below. A fresh volley of shots blew splinters from the balcony railing and punched holes in the wall and ceiling.

"How's your ammo?" Ronnie asked.

"One more mag."

"Me too. I vote we go up. We're too exposed."

"After you, my man."

"Coming up," Ronnie called.

They ran up the stairs. Elizabeth waited at the top.

"How many?" she asked.

"I don't know. Wish I had a grenade," Ronnie said.

"Can't be many more," Lamont said. "We already took out at least six."

Ronnie looked around. A large sideboard stood against one wall in the hallway. He went over to it.

"Lamont. Help me move this."

The two men manhandled the heavy sideboard to the stairs. They tipped it onto its side to make a barricade across the stairs.

"Better than nothing," Ronnie said.

"We can't stay up here," Lamont said. "They'll figure something out. We have to take it to them."

"How you want to do that?"

"We climb down that big drainpipe on the side of the building and come up behind them."

"Lamont," Elizabeth said. "Go after them. We can hold them off. Go through the kitchen and grab the shotgun."

A Remington 870 was mounted on the wall in the pantry. With the sporting plug removed, it held five rounds of double ought buck, nine pellets to a cartridge. It was a formidable weapon at close quarters.

Freddie's voice boomed out again, but this time he was speaking in Japanese.

"What did he say?" Ronnie asked.

"Who cares," Lamont said. "Let's go."

They ran to the end of the hall and into Stephanie's bedroom. Ronnie opened a window. The drainpipe ran down the corner of the house, a foot away from the open window. Ronnie crawled out of the window and reached for the drainpipe with his left hand. He gripped the pipe and moved across, then got his other hand and his feet wrapped around it. He started shimmying down. Lamont followed. In a minute, they were on the ground outside the house.

They heard shouting and the staccato sound of automatic weapons inside, mixed with the single shots of pistols. There wasn't much time before the women would be overwhelmed.

The back door that led to a mudroom and the kitchen stood open. They ran in, pistols ready. Ronnie opened the pantry door and grabbed the shotgun, racking a round into the chamber.

He handed his pistol to Lamont. "Take this."

More shots sounded from above. Someone yelled in pain. It sounded like Stephanie or Elizabeth.

Ronnie took the lead with the shotgun. Lamont came close behind. They ran into the atrium, stepped over a body, and started up the stairs. Blood trickled down the steps from the dead men lying there. A man stood at the bottom of the stairway to the third floor, looking up at whatever was happening above. He turned as Ronnie reached the balcony level and shouted a warning. The blast of the Remington cut his shout short.

Ronnie ran forward, and looked up into the stairwell. Three of the intruders were at the top of the stairs, pushing the sideboard aside. Two lay dead on the stairs. Elizabeth and Stephanie were nowhere in sight.

Ronnie pointed the shotgun up the stairwell and began firing. He worked the pump until the gun was empty.

A load of double ought buck creates a cloud of death. It will rip through anything and everything before it. The lead balls shredded the men in the stairwell. Their screams blended with the blasts of the shotgun. It was a slaughter.

Everything went quiet.

"Director," Ronnie called. "You all right?"

"I'm fine. Steph's been hit."

"Shit," Ronnie said.

He went up the stairs. The walls and floor at the top of the stairs were covered with blood. Bodies lay crumpled on the steps. They were all Japanese.

Lamont came up behind Ronnie.

"Man, that shotgun makes a hell of a mess," he said.

They pushed what was left of the sideboard aside. It was splintered and broken, riddled with bullet holes and peppered with buckshot. Stephanie sat against the wall down the hall. Blood covered her white blouse. Elizabeth knelt next to her.

"It's only a flesh wound," she said.

"Let me see," Ronnie said.

The bullet had taken a piece out of the upper part of Steph's left arm. It was bleeding dark red.

"Looks like it missed the artery," Ronnie said.

He applied pressure to stop the bleeding.

"Lamont, grab a kit from the bathroom. In the cabinet, under the sink."

Half an hour later, they were trying to explain what had happened to the police.

THIRTY-TWO

"Yamamoto-san, the director of the American CIA is on line one."

Yamamoto picked up the phone.

"Clarence, how are you?"

"I'm fine, Daichi. I'm calling because there have been some developments here that directly concern you."

"Oh?"

"A yakuza assassination team attempted to kill Elizabeth Harker and the rest of her team last night."

"Ah. I hope they were unsuccessful?"

"They were. Unfortunately, all of them are dead. We identified one as a man named Genki Watanabe. We believe he was the leader. Do you know who this man was?"

"Eeeeee. I am truly amazed at what your people have done," Yamamoto said. "Watanabe was boss of Kobayashi's East Coast operations in your country. He was the equivalent of Tanaka. By killing these two men, a serious blow has been dealt to Kobayashi's prestige and standing. Are you aware of what happened in the museum yesterday?"

"No one has briefed me on that."

"Kobayashi attempted to assassinate Carter and Doctor Connor while they were in the National Museum. She took a sword from a display case and cut the man down. It has created quite a stir here."

"You can't be serious. She killed him with a sword?"

"I assure you, Clarence, I am quite serious. More, she did it using a famous sword. According to legend, the sword is cursed and requires periodic feedings of blood. Our media is in a complete frenzy."

"A cursed sword? This is turning into something like one of your Noh plays."

"I fear these setbacks to Kobayashi will incite a yakuza war here. There are many who would like to take Kobayashi's place. His failure to kill his enemies and the loss of two chief lieutenants are serious humiliations for him. They will be perceived as weakness. Kobayashi's leadership is at stake. He will not go easily."

"That Masamune sword has caused many problems."

"There will be more," Yamamoto said. "I am sure this is only the beginning. You are not Japanese, Clarence. Your thinking about these events will be shadowed by our cultural differences. For us, such a powerful symbol as the sword has a way of creating its own reality. It becomes an object around which events circle until there is a resolution."

"What kind of resolution?"

"That I cannot tell you. If I am successful, resolution means the sword will take its rightful place among our other national treasures."

"And if you are not?"

"I prefer to think the outcome will be as I desire. To that end, I would like for your people to remain here in Japan for the near future."

"You want Nick and Selena to stay? What do you have in mind for them?"

"This all began because Nobuyasu hired them to find the sword. They have now become a lightning rod for Kobayashi. That makes them valuable to Nobuyasu."

"How so?"

"Kobayashi is attempting to force the Black Swan Society and the keiretsu to back his candidate for premier in the next election. He is using Nobuyasu's desire to obtain the Masamune sword as leverage to force their agreement. The society will follow Nobuyasu's lead. I know Nobuyasu. He will never allow Kobayashi to dominate him, sword or no sword."

"What does this have to do with Nick and Selena?"

"Kobayashi is obsessed with getting revenge upon them. He must do so to restore confidence in his leadership. The yakuza society is like a small village. Nothing can be hidden, everything is known. Time is running out for Kobayashi, and he knows it."

"Go on."

"Nick is the one who killed Tanaka. What do you think would happen if Nobuyasu told Kobayashi he could give him Nick in exchange for the sword?

"You want to use him as bait? I can't countenance that, Daichi."

"I have discussed this with him and he is willing."

"Nick has always been a little hotheaded. He has an emotional investment in this."

Sitting at his desk on the seventh floor at Langley, Clarence thought about Yamamoto's suggestion. The body count had been rising since the discovery of the sword. Kobayashi had proved to be a dangerous and relentless adversary. Unless he was stopped, the lives of Nick and Selena, Elizabeth and the others would continue to be at risk.

Elizabeth.

She could have been killed when Watanabe's men attacked. Unbidden, an image flashed across his mind of her broken body lying in a pool of blood, murdered by fanatical criminals who covered their bodies in tattoos. He shuddered.

"Tell me your plan," he said.

THIRTY-THREE

Atagi Nobuyasu was reading about the incident in the museum. It was inconceivable that a foreigner and a woman could have done what she did. The picture accompanying the article showed Selena as she was about to deliver the blow that had cut her opponent in half.

With grudging admiration, Nobuyasu noted her stance, her grip on the sword, her intense and focused energy. Perhaps she had been samurai in some previous incarnation. How else to explain what had happened?

Too bad it wasn't Kobayashi that had died.

Kobayashi.

Thinking about the betrayal of the yakuza chief was keeping Atagi up at night. He had discussed Kobayashi's demands with the rest of the council in the society. As expected, blame for the unfortunate turn of events had been laid at his feet. No one was willing to accept Kobayashi's alternative candidate. It had been made clear to Atagi that he needed to find a solution to the problem, but the solution remained elusive.

As if that wasn't enough, he was under a lot of pressure from his creditors. The window for avoiding financial disaster was closing. Time was running out. If his candidate wasn't elected, he'd be ruined. Anger and worry were affecting his judgment. Something needed to be done, and soon. But what?

His phone rang, the one with the private number given only to a few. He looked at the display.

The American, Harker. What does she want?

"Yes."

"Nobuyasu-san, this is Nick Carter. You remember who I am?"

"What do you want, Carter?"

Atagi saw no reason to be polite. Because of Carter, Kobayashi had the sword.

"I have a proposition for you," Nick said. "How would you like to get the sword from Kobayashi? Maybe eliminate him at the same time?"

"You had the sword. Now you don't. I am not impressed."

"Nobuyasu-san, you need to hear me out. There is something Kobayashi wants more than he wants the sword."

"Oh? What would that be?"

"Me. He wants revenge for the death of his lieutenants. Suppose he thought you were holding me prisoner. You could tell him you would exchange me for the sword. I have caused him a lot of trouble. It makes him look weak. The sharks are circling, and he has to do something to regain respect. From what I know of your culture, that is more important to him than anything else."

"You would act as bait?"

"That's right."

"Why would you do this?"

"I want a million dollars, deposited in an account in the Caymans. The sword is worth a lot more than that."

"Your wife is rich. Why would you need money?"

"My wife is a pain in the ass. She controls all the money. I'm tired of having to ask when I want to buy something. You're a rich man. A million is nothing to you."

Greedy barbarian, Nobuyasu thought with contempt. *He has no honor.*

"What do you say?" Nick said.

"I will think about it and call you when I have made a decision."

"Don't wait too long."

Nick disconnected.

"You played that well," Yamamoto said.

Nick and Selena were in Yamamoto's office at public security headquarters. The conversation had been on speaker phone.

"The hook is set. If he wasn't interested, he would have hung up on me."

"He didn't balk when you asked for a million dollars," Yamamoto said.

"That's another reason I think he's in play. Now we wait for him to contact me. He'll call back soon, I'm certain."

"So I'm a pain in the ass now?" Selena said.

"I had to make up something. He knows you have a lot of money. He wants that sword badly enough that he's not going to question my motivation. He thinks all foreigners lack honor. By asking for money, I confirmed his belief."

"If he agrees, you are placing yourself in a very dangerous situation," Yamamoto said. "As you said, he thinks you are unworthy. He has no respect for you. That makes you expendable. Once he has what he wants, he will kill you. It will happen at the exchange."

"Lots of people have tried to kill me, but I'm still here. He'll try to kill Kobayashi as well. Kobayashi is going to want to kill him. It should be an interesting meeting."

"You always did have a gift for understatement," Selena said.

"We should discuss what we want to do if he agrees," Yamamoto said.

"I can see one problem right away," Nick said. "We don't know where the meeting will take place. Once I'm in Nobuyasu's hands, he's not going to let me make any calls."

"We'll plant a tracker on you," Yamamoto said.

"I'd be surprised if he doesn't check for that."

"He can check all he wants. This is new technology we developed."

Yamamoto reached into a drawer in his desk and took out a tiny object, smaller than a grain of rice.

"This uses nanotechnology," he's said. "It is not detectable by the devices that are normally available. It has a range of one thousand meters. We will know where you are at all times and where they are taking you."

"They'll search me."

"They won't find it. Swallow it before they come to get you."

He placed the tracker in a small plastic bag and gave it to Nick. Then he entered a command on his computer keyboard. A map grid with coordinates appeared with a green, flashing dot.

Yamamoto pointed at the dot. "That's you. Or it will be, once you swallow it."

Nick took the tracker and put it in his jacket pocket.

"I'm assigning a team of six men to you," Yamamoto said. "These are my most experienced operatives. They will be armed and nearby at all times. Once you arrive at the meeting location, Kobayashi and Nobuyasu will not be able to resist spending time insulting each other while pretending to negotiate. That is when we will move in."

"You think six will be enough? What about backup?"

"There will be a police helicopter standing by. We'll send it up once we know where you're going. Our SWAT teams are very good."

"I don't like this, Nick," Selena said.

"I thought we'd agreed this was the best course of action."

"You never asked me if I thought it was a good idea or not. What if something goes wrong? What if that tracker doesn't work, or we lose the signal? What if Kobayashi or Nobuyasu do something we don't expect?"

"We have to do this," Nick said. "If we don't, Kobayashi and his goons are going to keep after us. They almost killed everyone back in Virginia. One of these times they'll succeed, if we don't get them first."

"I suppose you're right. But I still don't like it."

"I'll be all right."

"I wish we'd never seen that sword," Selena said.

"Are you sure you want to go through with this?" Yamamoto said.

"Like I said, I have to."

Good, Yamamoto thought.

THIRTY-FOUR

Nobuyasu called back early in the evening on the same day.

"Yes," Nick answered.

"Your proposal has merit," Nobuyasu said.

"I want half the money up front."

"That can be arranged."

Nick gave him an account number.

"When I see the money is there, we can meet and discuss how you want this to happen."

"Very well. I will call you in one hour."

Nobuyasu disconnected.

Nick turned to Selena. "He went for it."

Next he called Yamamoto and told him Nobuyasu was in play.

"I'm going to swallow the tracker," Nick said. "Let me know how it shows up on your screen."

He washed the tracker down with a gulp of water.

"I'm still reading a strong signal," Yamamoto said. "We're good for a day or so."

"This should all be over long before then," Nick said.

Exactly one hour later, Nobuyasu called.

"You have confirmed the deposit?"

"Yes, I can see that it's there."

"A car will pick you up. Fifteen minutes."

Nobuyasu disconnected.

"He's sending a car," Nick said to Selena. "I'll let Yamamoto know."

Ten minutes later, Nick was standing in front of the hotel, waiting for Nobuyasu's car. He was unarmed, except for a ceramic blade hidden in the lining of his jacket. It wouldn't register on a scanner. A pat down search would be unlikely to find it. It wasn't much, but it was better than nothing.

A sleek Mercedes limousine with blacked out windows pulled up to the curb. A large man got out of the back, leaving the door open. He was at least two hundred and fifty pounds, with short cropped hair and a head that reminded Nick of a particularly ugly bowling ball. His jacket struggled to contain his broad shoulders. His expression was unfriendly. He gestured for Nick to raise his arms and passed an electronic wand around his body. Then he pushed Nick toward the car.

Nick put away second thoughts about what he was doing. He got in the car.

Another large man sat in the back against the door. The first man got in after Nick, sandwiching him in the middle. He pulled the door closed after him. The car moved away from the hotel. The first man turned and smiled, then drove his elbow into Nick's stomach. Nick doubled over, gasping for air. Both men began punching him. One of them brought a fist down on the back of his head. Everything went dark.

When he came to, he was lying on a concrete floor in a windowless room. His body ached all over from the beating he'd taken. He was still wearing his jacket. It was torn and dirty.

It took a moment to gather his wits.

Bastards really worked me over. I hope that tracker is working. I hope Yamamoto's men are nearby.

He sat up against the wall and took in the room. It was small, like a large storage closet. There was a single door, closed. He looked for a camera but didn't see one.

They're improvising.

With an effort, he rose to his feet and leaned against the wall. His knee was sore and swollen. It felt like it might give out. His back hurt like hell, right where he'd gotten injured during the jump into Tibet, years ago. He probed his teeth with his tongue. One of them felt loose. One eye was almost shut. His face was sticky with dried blood.

Not winning any beauty contests today.

Nick felt the lining of his jacket for his knife, found it, and freed it up. He slipped the blade into his pocket, just as the lock on the door turned. The door opened. Nobuyasu stood there with bowling ball man next to him.

"Ah, you are up. Good."

"This wasn't part of the deal," Nick said.

"I suggest you be quiet," Nobuyasu said. "You are still alive because I need you for Kobayashi. If you cooperate, I may allow you to live."

"I thought your code of honor would prevent you from doing something like this."

"Honor is something that goes with respect. You do not deserve respect. You are no better than a thief. A man who acts as you have, for money, has no honor and deserves none. Kobayashi will expect to find you like this. After all, realism is essential if he is to believe I kidnapped you so I could offer to exchange you for the sword. He would never believe you would come willingly."

"You gain nothing by killing me. My friends will never rest until they take you down."

"Do you seriously think I'm concerned about the people you call your friends? Please, Carter, don't insult my intelligence. I'm going to leave you now and call Kobayashi."

He gestured at the huge man standing next to him.

"Kento will be here outside the door, in case you have second thoughts about cooperating. His grandparents were killed by your B-29s in the war. He hates Americans. Do I make myself clear?"

"Yes."

"Good."

Nobuyasu said something in Japanese to Kento, who turned to look at Nick, and scowled.

The door closed, leaving Nick to his thoughts.

Nobuyasu went upstairs and called Kobayashi.

"You have the American?"

"Yes. He's a little worse for wear, but still in fine shape. You can make an example of him. That should go a long way toward restoring faith in your leadership, *oyabun*."

Nobuyasu's voice conveyed his contempt.

Kobayashi gave no sign that he'd registered the insult. There would be time to deal with it later.

"There is an abandoned tuna factory in Chiba City on the waterfront," he said. "No one goes there after dark. We will make the exchange there."

"I know where it is," Nobuyasu said.

"Bring the American. I will bring the sword. Eleven tonight."

THIRTY-FIVE

The tracker inside Nick's gut worked perfectly. Yamamoto's men were watching the building where Nick was being held, a private house in the exclusive Abazu district, one of Nobuyasu's many properties.

Kanamoto Fujita was in charge of Yamamoto's team. His orders were to observe only, unless he saw Kobayashi arrive. Nothing would happen until Nobuyasu and Kobayashi met. It was reasonable to assume Nick was safe until the time and place of the exchange.

Fujita's companion in the car was an old friend, Masataka Kagura. The two had known each other since they'd gone through initial training with the agency. Kagura sat behind the wheel, observing the house through binoculars.

"Mas, something's happening," Kagura said. "The front door is opening."

A Mercedes limo was parked in front of the house. They watched Nobuyasu's men come out with Nick between them. He was limping.

Kagura adjusted the focus.

"Looks like they worked him over."

"It figures. Nobuyasu is a real bastard."

"Here comes the man himself."

Nobuyasu came out and got into the front seat of the Mercedes. The others crowded into the back. The Mercedes pulled away from the curb.

"Lock and load," Kagura said.

Fujita sighed. "You have been watching too many American movies."

Kagura waited until the limo was down the street and then pulled out after them. The second team car followed. Fujita spoke into his headset. It connected him back to headquarters, where Yamamoto was monitoring the operation.

"They're on the way," he said.

"I've got them on the monitor," Yamamoto said. "Good hunting."

"Copy," Fujita said.

"Let me guess," Kagura said. "He said 'good hunting.'"

"He can't help himself. I think he misses being out in the field."

"Must be tough, sitting in that big office all day."

"Come on, you know better than that. Would you want his job?"

"Not a chance."

The Mercedes took an on-ramp to the Higashi-Kantō Expressway.

"Where are they going?"

"Can't tell yet. It's too soon."

The Expressway roughly parallelled the coast of Tokyo Bay and passed through several cities. Nobuyasu could be headed almost anywhere. Forty minutes and several toll stations later, they knew his destination.

"Chiba City," Fujita said into his microphone. "They're headed for the waterfront."

"Stay with them," Yamamoto said. "Remember. Don't let anything happen to the American."

This part of Tokyo was known as the Keiyō industrial zone, a broad concentration of heavy industry spread along the northeast coast of the bay.

"Douse the lights," Fujita said. "Fall back a little. We can't let them see us."

After a few minutes, Kagura pointed ahead.

"I think they're going to the old tuna plant. There's nothing else down here. This whole area is up for redevelopment."

Fujita relayed the information back to headquarters. They followed the taillights of Nobuyasu's limo until the shadowed outline of the deserted building emerged from the darkness. The Mercedes' brake lights flared red. The limo pulled up by the entrance to the plant. Another Mercedes was parked there, empty. It didn't look as though anyone else was around.

"They're definitely going into the old tuna plant," Fujita said into his microphone.

"I'm releasing the helicopter now," Yamamoto said.

Kagura eased the car to a stop. The second car pulled in behind them. The men got out.

"Check your weapons," Fujita said.

THIRTY-SIX

Nick felt the comforting shape of the ceramic blade in his pocket as Nobuyasu's thugs marched him into the cavernous building. Silvery moonlight poured through broken skylights high above, casting dim shadows about the abandoned factory. Everywhere he looked, rusting machinery stood silent witness to outdated technology. They walked along a silent beltway that had once moved boxes filled with cans of tuna to the loading dock for shipment. Nick thought he heard a soft footfall somewhere behind them, but he couldn't be sure.

Something scuttled away in the dark.

Rats. I hate rats.

Cold, bright light shone in the darkness ahead. They turned a corner and came into a large open area.

At one time the space had been a cafeteria. Puddles of rainwater and trash littered the area. There were still dozens of tables and chairs, scattered about on a cracked, tile floor. Kobayashi and three of his men waited on the other side of a hissing gas lantern in the middle of the room. The titanium case containing the Masamune sword lay on one of the tables.

Showtime, Nick thought.

His ear began itching.

The shit's about to hit the fan, and all I've got is a four inch piece of ceramic.

The thug called Kento gripped Nick's left arm. The other man had gone to stand by his boss. The lantern cast a ghoulish circle of light on the floor. It shone up onto the men standing around the lantern, distorting their faces with black shadows. They looked like characters in a grade B horror movie.

To Nick's right was the old cafeteria food counter. A triple rail of rusting chrome ran in front of it, where the workers had moved trays along as they made their choices. To the left was darkness. Above, broken skylights revealed the night sky.

"Let me see the sword," Nobaysau said.

"All of this could have been avoided," Kobayashi said. "If you and your friends in the society had seen reason about our candidate, we would not be standing here now."

"No one would vote for the idiot you proposed," Nobuyasu said. "He's a drunk and a yakuza pawn. It all would have come out in the election."

"You forget, my clan controls the media. It would not have come out. The keiretsu are powerful, but it is no longer up to them to choose who leads our nation. You and your friends must learn to cooperate with us."

"We had an agreement. You are the one who broke it, by proposing your ridiculous candidate. We were willing to cooperate, but now things are different."

"Yes, they are."

Kobayashi snapped his fingers. A half
dozen men with submachine guns emerged
from the darkness on Nick's left.

"Kobayashi, you disappoint me,"
Nobuyasu said. "Did you think I wouldn't be
prepared for more of your treachery?"

He raised his hand in the air. More men
appeared from a different direction. They,
too, were armed with machine pistols.

Shit, Nick thought. *How did these guys
get in here? How come I didn't hear them?*

"We seem to be in a standoff,"
Nobuyasu said. "Give me the sword. I will
give you the American. We can all leave
here to live another day. But first, let me see
it. I'm sure you understand I don't have
much reason to trust you, Kobayashi-san."

"The case has not been opened,"
Kobayashi said. "It has a biometric lock on
it. The American brought it here. He will be
able to open it."

Nobuyasu looked at Nick.

"Can you open the case? Think, before
you answer."

"Yes," Nick said. "I can open it."

"Kento," Nobuyasu said.

The man Nick still thought of as
bowling ball man grunted and pushed Nick
toward the table where the box with the
sword lay. As he approached the table, Nick
saw Kobayashi looking at him, his face
calm, his eyes gleaming black with anger.

"I look forward to our time together,"
he said. "You have caused me a lot of
trouble."

"You shouldn't have come after my friends," Nick said.

"Open the case," Nobuyasu called.

Nick pressed his left thumb on the biometric lock. There was an audible click as the case unlocked. As it did, Nick pulled the ceramic knife from his pocket and jammed it into Kento's neck.

The big Japanese staggered back, clutching his neck. Blood spurted out between his fingers.

Nick flipped open the lid of the box, grabbed the sword, and swung it backhanded at Kobayashi. The blade caught him across the face and slashed through his cheeks, coming out on the other side.

Kobayashi screamed and grabbed at his face with both hands.

Someone fired the first shot. The room filled with the sound of automatic weapons. Hundreds of empty casings scattered over the hard floor, bouncing from the tiles.

In the shadows, Fujita and his men had been watching.

"Holy shit," he said. "Go. Go. "

They ran forward and began firing, adding to the confusion. Nick turned, the sword in his hand, when something hit him hard in the back of the head. He fell to the floor. The sword slid across the tiles.

Nobuyasu ran forward in a crouch, picked up the weapon and disappeared into the darkness of the abandoned building. The last thing Nick heard before everything faded was the sound of helicopter blades beating against the night.

THIRTY-SEVEN

Nick opened his eyes. His head hurt. He had a pounding headache. He lay flat on his back, looking up at the roof of the cannery.

Someone bent over him, a Japanese man.

"Nick-san, are you all right?"

Nick sat up. The pounding in his head got worse. He closed his eyes.

"Got a headache."

Nick put his hand up to the back of his head. It came away wet, sticky with blood. He looked at his hand, trying to make sense of what he saw.

"You were shot. The bullet grazed your head. You are very lucky man, Nick."

"Who are you?"

"I am Kanamoto Fujita. I work for Director Yamamoto."

It was hard to think. Memory returned, the sound of the sword hissing through the air, the splash of blood in the moonlight as the gleaming steel sliced through Kobayashi's face. Then, darkness.

"Where's the sword?"

"Gone," Fujita said. "Nobuyasu took it. He got away."

"Son of a bitch," Nick said. "We have to find him."

He started to stand. A wave of dizziness knocked him back down. Somewhere, sirens were coming closer.

"You must not try to get up," Fujita said. "An ambulance is coming."

Sudden nausea made Nick feel sick.

"Yeah, okay. You have to find the sword."

"We will. Please, lie down."

Nick lay back and closed his eyes, fighting the nausea.

The next time he opened his eyes, he was in a hospital bed. Selena sat in a chair nearby. His mind felt clear.

"Hey," he said.

"Hey, yourself."

She got up and sat on the bed, leaned over him. She wore no makeup. Her face was tired with worry and stress.

"You're all right," she said. "You have a concussion. The bullet bounced right off that hard skull of yours, you dumb idiot."

She started to cry. He reached up and pulled her down to him.

"Hey. Hey, it's all right. I'm here, aren't I? It takes more than a bunch of tattooed gangsters to kill me."

"Damn it, Nick."

"Shh, shhh. I'm okay. It's okay."

She sat up and brushed tears away. "No, it's not okay."

Selena got up and walked past Yamamoto as he came into the room. Nick watched her go. Yamamoto looked at her, then turned to Nick.

"Is everything all right?"

He took the chair that Selena had been sitting in.

"She's upset," Nick said.

"Ah. Yes, I understand."

"That meeting wasn't supposed to go like that," Nick said. "Have you found Nobuyasu?"

"No. He seems to have disappeared."

"Are you going to arrest him?"

Yamamoto looked uncomfortable.

"It isn't as simple as that. He is an important man. This is Japan, Nick. Things are always very complicated here."

"What do you mean? He's a crook. He was going to turn me over to Kobayashi to be killed."

"Yes, that's true. But as I said, it's complicated. Don't worry, we'll get him eventually. First we have to find him. By the way, Kobayashi is still alive. He will be badly disfigured, but he will live. You marked him for life. He's finished as obayun. The yakuza will fight among themselves for a while until a new leader emerges. Then things will go on as before."

"Not much changes, does it?"

"No. Some things always remain the same, even if the actors change. At least you no longer need concern yourself with these events. We will find Nobuyasu. When we do, we will recover the sword."

"Sounds good to me. I'll be happy if I never see it again."

"I hope you will stay in Japan a little while longer. There are many wonderful things to do and see here. I would like you to have better memories of my country than what you have experienced so far."

"Thank you, Yamamoto-san. It depends on what Selena wants to do, but I think we'll go home. We have children."

"Ah, of course, children. Well."

Yamamoto rose.

"It has been interesting working with you, Nick. You are welcome back at any time."

Yamamoto bowed. Nick inclined his head from where he lay propped up in the bed.

"If Selena is out there, would you send her in?"

"Hai."

Yamamoto left the room. A moment later Selena came in and sat on the bed.

"Nick..."

"I know. You don't have to say anything. Yamamoto suggested we hang around for a while and see the sights. I told him we needed to get home to the kids."

She leaned over and kissed him.

"They don't want to let you out of here for another day," she said. "I argued with them but they won't budge. Something about their responsibility under Japanese law."

"Another day won't matter. Besides have you seen the nurses here?"

"Stop trying to pretend you're Lamont," Selena said.

Nick realized he didn't even know what time it was, or what day.

"What time is it anyway?"

"It's five in the morning. They brought you straight here."

Nick yawned. His headache was still there.

"I guess I could use a day of taking it easy. What are you going to do today?"

"I'm going to go back to the hotel and sleep. After that, I'm coming here."

"Sounds like a plan."

Selena looked at him.

"They told me you were shot in the head. I thought you were going to die. Or that maybe you'd be a vegetable. Drooling."

"A drooling vegetable? That's a hell of an image. I'm sorry you had to go through this."

"I love you, Nick."

He took her hand.

"I love you too."

An attractive nurse came into the room as Selena bent down to kiss him.

"You have to go," she said. "He has to rest."

"See," Nick said. "Nurses."

"Smart ass. I'll be back in a few hours," Selena said.

THIRTY-EIGHT

On the outskirts of the city stood a traditional house surrounded by a high wall. After fleeing the chaos of the meeting in the cannery, Nobuyasu had come here with the sword. The property was heavily protected by his men and an advanced security system. There was no chance he'd be disturbed once he was inside the gate.

He sat cross-legged on a cushion and contemplated the Masamune sword. It lay on a low, polished table before him. He took deep breaths, forcing himself to be calm, still wired from the adrenaline charge of the events at the cannery.

There hadn't been time to take the scabbard, only enough time to pick up the blood-drenched sword and run. He'd washed the blade with clean, cold water and dried it with a silk cloth. Now it sat waiting for him.

Waiting to reveal its secret.

At last.

Over the years Nobuyasu had acquired many properties, old and new. He was particularly fond of older Japanese homes built in the traditional style. They suited his sense of traditional values. Of course they often required remodeling. He'd purchased one such home in Osaka several years before, not far from the famous castle built by Toyotomi Hideyoshi.

At the end of the sixteenth century, Hideyoshi had been the most powerful general in Japan, more powerful than the Emperor. The Masamune sword had been sold to the Toyotomi clan by the man who had won it in battle. After Hideyoshi's death and the eventual defeat of his son, the sword was sold to the Tokugawas.

The home where Nobuyasu sat contemplating the sword had once belonged to Hideyoshi's chief advisor. When the house was being remodeled workers discovered a secret compartment in the wall. It contained a scroll, a painting of Hideyoshi with the Masamune sword. The text on the scroll that had set Nobuyasu on the quest to find the sword.

As he neared death, Hideyoshi worried that the fate of his son and his clan were in jeopardy. Civil war was sure to begin when he died. Money would be needed to fend off the samurai of Iyeasu Togukawa and his allies.

A lot of money.

Hideyoshi stole funds marked for the armies in Korea and buried the treasure. It was an enormous sum, more than a hundred tons of gold. Over time, the treasure had become the stuff of legend. Every Japanese knew of the *Tenshou Ooban*. Historical records backed up the legends. The gold had existed. It had never reached Korea, and had never been found.

No one knew where it was, but Nobuyasu was about to find out. The scroll said that the secret to finding the treasure was hidden within the hilt of the Masamune sword.

Hideyoshi would have assumed the sword would never pass from his family's hands. It would have seemed a safe place to hide clues to the location of the treasure.

Oh, so clever, general, Nobuyasu thought. *Too clever for your own good. Your son was defeated before he could claim the gold, and the secret died with him.*

Nobuyasu picked up the sword. His hands trembled with excitement. Following directions from the scroll he'd memorized long ago, he pressed the decorative gold inlays on the hilt in a specific sequence.

One. Three. Three. Five. Seven. Two. Two. One. Nine.

The gold cap on the end of the hilt popped open. He peered inside and saw a roll of thin paper wrapped around the end of the tang. Carefully, he extracted the paper. It had been rolled up for a very long time, but Nobuyasu was patient and gentle. Soon it was laid out under a piece of glass. He bent down to read it, and cursed in frustration.

The faded characters inked on the paper made no sense. The writing looked like Japanese in the old style, but something wasn't right. It was a dialect, or it was in code, or both. Whatever it was, he couldn't read it.

Nobuyasu got up and went to a cabinet, took out a bottle of Johnny Walker Blue, and poured himself a large drink. He looked over at the sword lying on the table and the message under glass next to it. That piece of paper held his salvation. The gold would stave off financial ruin. He could use it to sway the next election.

The answer to all his problems was right there on that piece of paper, and he couldn't read it.

Nobuyasu drained his glass and filled it again. He couldn't take the paper to one of the experts in medieval Japanese. No one must know about it. No one could be trusted with information like that. No, the regular channels were out. Who could he get to read it?

When the answer came, he smiled at the perfect irony of it.

THIRTY-NINE

Selena slept for several hours, undisturbed in the quiet hotel room. She got out of bed, used the toilet, and got into the shower. The hot water felt wonderful, cascading over her hair and down her back, washing away the tension of the night before.

She finished showering, stepped out, and dried off. She wrapped her hair in a towel and put on one of the hotel's thick robes. She went back into the bedroom, picked up the hotel phone and ordered room service. She was told it would be about thirty minutes.

No problem. It would give her time to get ready. Once she'd eaten, she was going to the hospital to see Nick. He was being discharged today. She was looking forward to getting home and seeing the twins. It was a relief to know that all the problems surrounding the sword were no longer her concern.

She applied a little makeup and dressed in a pair of loose black slacks, a navy blue blouse and comfortable black shoes. As she finished she heard a knock on the door.

"Who is it?" she called.

"Room service."

Good. I'm starved.

As she started to open the door, it slammed into her and knocked her down. Two big men swarmed over her. One of them pressed a cloth to her face. A sweet, sick smell filled her nostrils as she struggled. Then she was gone.

When she awoke, she was lying on her side on a futon. Her hands were numb. Her feet were bound at the ankles. A wave of nausea hit her. She leaned over the edge and vomited. She waited for the nausea and dizziness to pass, then levered herself up to a sitting position.

Selena took in the room, wondering where she was. She couldn't hear any traffic. There were no windows. The only piece of furniture was the futon. There was one door, closed, probably locked. There was nothing in the room she could use as a weapon.

Whoever had tied her up had done a good job, using several ties. Selena could get out of one, but three were too many. If she struggled, the ties would bind more tightly.

She was at the mercy of whoever had taken her.

When Nick discovered she was gone, he'd come after her. She knew he'd find her. The question was whether or not he'd be in time. Whoever was willing to do this wasn't likely to let her live after he'd gotten whatever he wanted from her.

She heard a key in the lock on the door. The tumblers clicked and the door opened. Nobuyasu stood in the doorway, one of his large bodyguards behind him.

"Excellent. I see you are awake."

"You have no idea what kind of trouble you've made for yourself."

Nobuyasu laughed.

"Oh, I'm not worried, Doctor Connor. No one will ever be able to prove I am responsible for your disappearance. Your husband is still in the hospital. My men are watching him. If you would like him to remain unharmed, you will do as I say. You are probably hoping he will come after you. There's no trail for him to follow when he gets out. No, I'm afraid you are entirely on your own. It's up to you whether he lives or dies, and whether you have an easy time here or something quite a bit more difficult."

"What do you want, Atagi?"

"What do I want?"

Something in Nobuyasu's expression made Selena shudder. Something in his eyes.

Damn. He's insane.

"What do I want?" he said again. "I want you to read something for me. Do what I ask without giving me trouble, and I will let you go once we're done."

Sure, and I'm the Queen of England.

"Read something? What is it?"

"A very old document. It seems to be written in a dialect, or it could possibly be in code. Either way, I know you are one of the world's experts on things like this. That is why I brought you here."

Selena decided she'd pretend to cooperate. She'd get nowhere by challenging him.

"You could have asked," she said, in a neutral tone.

"After the events at the cannery, that wasn't an option," Nobuyasu said. "I regret that I have to engage your services in such an unpleasant way."

"You don't give me any choice," Selena said. "Promise me you won't go after Nick and I'll help you."

"I thought you would see things my way, Doctor Connor. You are an intelligent woman. It's the only rational response."

"You are descended from samurai. Give me your word of honor Nick will not be harmed. Otherwise I won't cooperate."

"I can make you cooperate."

"You can make me tell you things. You won't know if what I'm telling you is the truth. Promise."

Nobuyasu sighed. "Very well, I promise."

"On your honor."

"On my honor, I promise I won't harm him."

"All right. Where is this document?"

"In the other room."

"Would you please untie my feet? Otherwise you'll have to get one of your goons to carry me."

"I'm aware of your abilities in the martial arts," Nobuyasu said. "Any attempt to escape or attack me or my men will result in the death of your husband. You understand?"

"I understand."

Selena dropped her eyes and slumped, as if defeated.

Nobuyasu turned to his guard. "Untie her feet."

"My hands are numb," Selena said. "I can't feel my fingers. Please untie my hands also. You've made it clear what you'll do. I won't give you any trouble."

Nobuyasu considered. "Remember. No tricks. By the way, I know where your children are. Be sure to consider your actions."

Adrenaline and anger surged in her body. It took all her skill to hide what she was thinking.

You bastard. You're a dead man.

The bodyguard came over to her, took out a sharp knife, bent down and cut the zip ties from her ankles and wrists. She tried to stand but her feet had no feeling. Then her fingers and toes began to hurt as blood rushed back into them. Her fingers had turned white and she couldn't move them. She rubbed her hands back and forth against each other in an awkward motion, trying to bring back circulation.

"Genki, help her. Come, Doctor Connor."

Genki gripped her arms and helped her stand.

Nick, I hope you're on your way, she thought.

FORTY

"Taken? What do you mean, taken?"

Nick was dressed, getting ready to leave the hospital. Yamamoto stood near the bed, clearly unhappy about what he had to say.

"What I said, Nick. Somebody took her from your room at the hotel. She'd ordered room service. Your wife probably opened the door to her kidnappers. There were signs of a struggle and we found a rag soaked with chloroform. We think they knocked her out and got her out of the hotel in a laundry cart, by way of the service elevator."

"Why? Why would anybody want to kidnap her?"

Yamamoto shrugged. "I don't know. She is wealthy. Perhaps for ransom?"

"You don't believe that any more than I do," Nick said. "This must have something to do with that damn sword."

"You think Nobuyasu is responsible?"

"I think that's a good bet. Kobayashi is out of commission. The rest of the yakuza are busy trying to figure out who's going to take over. They're not going to waste time with us, not now. It has to be Nobuyasu."

"But why?"

"I don't know. We find him, my bet is we find Selena. And before you say anything, I'm not going home without her."

"You have no authority here, Nick-san."

"Then why don't you get me some, Yamamoto-san? Make me a temporary agent or something."

"This is not possible."

"You can make it possible. Look, I know I can't go blundering around looking for her. I need your help. But I can help you."

"How can you help us? You don't speak the language."

"I don't have to speak the language. I know how she thinks. She'll find a way to escape, or help us figure out where she is. She won't give up. Please, Yamamoto-san. I can get help from Director Harker. We have a lot of resources I can bring to the search. Satellite coverage, analysis, more."

"We have our own resources, Nick."

"I don't mean to imply that you don't, but I'm sure there are many demands on them. Why not let us help? We can focus entirely on finding Selena. You can't do that, but we can."

"If you stay, you must follow my instructions. No cowboy tactics, as you Americans like to say."

"No problem. Whatever you want."

Yamamoto considered, made up his mind.

"All right."

"Thank you, Yamamoto-san." Nick gave a short bow. "I need access to your files on Nobuyasu. Is that possible?"

"I'm sorry, I can't give you full access. But if you have specific questions, perhaps they can be answered."

Okay, Nick thought. *If that's how you want to play it. Freddie won't have any problem with your files. Probably best if I don't mention that.*

"I understand. Where do you think Nobuyasu went after the cannery?"

"We are working on it. Unfortunately, there are many places where he might be. He owns many buildings throughout the city and nearby."

"Can I get a list of those properties?"

"Of course. I can have it to you within an hour."

"Then let's begin. I'll go back to the hotel and bring Director Harker up to speed. Can you have the list brought to me there?"

"I can."

"Then I'd better get going," Nick said.

Half an hour later he was in his room at the hotel. He called Elizabeth and told her what had happened.

"I need help, Director. Yamamoto's a bureaucrat. By the time I get what I need, Selena could be dead."

"What do you want me to do, Nick?"

"I want Freddie to hack into Yamamoto's files."

Stephanie was sitting nearby, listening to the conversation on speaker phone.

"What is it you need, Nick?" she said.

"Yamamoto has files on Nobuyasu he won't show me. I want to know what's in them."

I will be happy to assist, Nick.

"Thanks, Freddie, I knew you would."

"What else do you need?" Elizabeth asked.

"A weapon."

"Nick, you don't have any authority over there."

"So everyone keeps telling me."

"Let Yamamoto handle it."

"I don't trust him. He keeps reminding me about how important Nobuyasu is and how things are different here in Japan. I smell a rat."

"You think he'll protect Nobuyasu at the expense of Selena?"

"Call it a hunch, but that's exactly what I think. I need a weapon."

"Nick..."

"Director, this is Selena we're talking about. Nobuyasu could do anything. You didn't see him over here, like I did. I think he's losing it."

My analysis indicates Yamamoto will not act with sufficient speed to resolve the situation without damage to Selena. There is a ninety-four point two percent chance that a successful conclusion depends upon Nick's intervention.

"I heard that," Nick said.

"All right, Nick," Elizabeth said. "I'll talk to DCI Hood and see if he can get a pistol to you."

"Yamamoto can't know about this."

"Don't worry, Nick," Elizabeth said. "This isn't my first rodeo."

FORTY-ONE

Nobuyasu led Selena to a large room near the front of the house. It was Japanese style, the floor covered with tightly woven tatami mats. Shoji screens stood open onto a classic Japanese garden surrounded by a high, stone wall. A soothing sound of running water came from the garden. A low table and several cushions were placed in the middle of the room. The Masamune sword lay on another table near one wall.

Too far away to reach. I'd never make it.

She looked out at the garden. "This is a beautiful spot. It's very peaceful."

"You appreciate the garden?"

"How could one not appreciate beauty such as this?"

"My experience is that Westerners are incapable of seeing the subtleties of our gardens."

Selena decided to ignore the insult.

"Where is this document you want me to look at?"

"On the table," Nobuyasu said. "Under that piece of glass."

Selena sat on a cushion and rubbed her hands together. Feeling had returned, along with an intense burning sensation. She looked at the document.

"At first glance this looks like it's written in late middle Japanese. But it's not quite right."

"Even I could determine that, Doctor Connor."

"I need a computer and access to the Internet."

"I don't think that would be a good idea," Nobuyasu said. "What's to prevent you from contacting your friends?"

"You'll be standing right over my shoulder. You implied that you would harm my children. I believe you. I won't risk that."

"You are wise to believe me"

"I need to compare the structures of middle Japanese and late middle Japanese. They're different, and I need a computer to do it properly. Looking at this document, I can see things in the grammatical structure that shouldn't be there. I suspect this is written in a combination of the two, and the combination used as the basis of a private code. That would explain why at first glance it appears to be gibberish."

"You cannot do this without a computer?"

"No. I don't have my references here, the way I would back home. Besides, I'd use a computer there as well. What's so important about this document anyway?"

"You don't need to know that."

He turned away.

"Genki, there is a laptop in my study. Bring it here."

"Hai."

Genki left the room. Moments later he returned with the laptop.

"Put it on the table."

Selena opened the computer and turned it on.

"Remember, Doctor Connor. The lives of your husband and your children are at stake. Do not make a mistake."

"You can watch what I do," Selena said. "I told you, I believe you."

She watched the screen boot. In the lower corner, an icon popped up that told her she was now connected to the Internet.

Got you, asshole, she thought.

She entered a search string for late middle Japanese and a short string of commands.

"What are you searching for?"

The screen lit with a British Museum page about the Japanese language.

"This," Selena said.

In Virginia, Elizabeth was sitting at her desk. Lamont and Ronnie were in the room with her. She called Hood, but he'd told her he couldn't get a weapon to Nick.

"I don't like refusing, Elizabeth, but I have to be careful," he said. "An international incident with Japan at this time would be a disaster. They're building up their military and the president is negotiating to sell them our latest fighter aircraft. It's important nothing interferes with that."

Elizabeth suppressed her anger. It felt like a betrayal.

"I understand, Clarence."

"Whatever he does, tell him not to get caught."

Hood disconnected.

"No good. He won't help."

"Send us over there, director," Ronnie said.

Freddie's voice sounded through the speakers in her office.

Director, I have received a message from Selena.

"A message? What does it say?"

It does not specifically say anything.

"Then how is it a message, Freddie?"

She included a protocol to connect with me in a search string she entered on the computer she is using. I have been able to identify her location and tap into her computer as she works at it. She is comparing two variations of Japanese language that precede modern usage.

"You have an address? Her location?"

That is correct.

"What is it?"

Freddie recited an address in the Chiba Prefecture.

"Excellent, Freddie. Please continue to monitor her actions."

Processing.

Elizabeth called Hood on his private line.

"Elizabeth, what is it?"

"I know where Selena is being held. I have the address. I need you to get hold of Yamamoto."

"Go ahead."

She gave him the information.

"I'll call him now," Hood said.

"Tell him to hurry," Elizabeth said.

FORTY-TWO

Nobuyasu watched Selena as she studied charts on the laptop comparing the structure of early and late medieval Japanese. He was growing impatient.

"Well? What have you found?"

"As I suspected, this document is a combination of two medieval variations of your language."

"Can you read it?"

"Not yet. It's in code, but I think I can break it."

"You need to hurry, Doctor Connor."

Selena looked up at him.

"You can't rush something like this. I think it's a substitution code, but I'm not certain. It's going to take me a while to figure it out."

"You can't read anything?"

"A few words. I can make out a reference to a castle at Osaka. Does that make sense to you?"

"There was a castle in Osaka, built by Hideyoshi. It has been restored as a symbol of our feudal past, but the original castle is gone. What does the document say about it?"

"I can't tell you that yet."

"Doctor Connor, let me remind you that the lives of your children and your husband are at stake."

"It won't do you any good to pressure me, Atagi."

"If I suspect that you are stalling, our pleasant collaboration will become more difficult. Do you understand?"

"Perfectly."

Selena turned back to the screen.

In spite of herself, she found herself drawn into the puzzle of decrypting the writing on the ancient piece of paper. She substituted different characters and rearranged words, using a system she'd developed years before for unraveling the secrets of dead languages.

Twenty minutes later, she had the first breakthrough. She looked up at Nobuyasu, who was standing nearby and looking over her shoulder.

"Maizoukin," she said. "This is about buried treasure, isn't it?"

"Very good, Doctor Connor."

"All these deaths? Because you're looking for some mythical treasure?"

"There's nothing mythical about it," Nobuyasu said. "No one knows where it was hidden, but this paper you are deciphering will tell me where it is."

"Where did you get this document from?"

"There's no harm in telling you. It was hidden in the hilt of the sword."

"So that's why you wanted it." Selena looked at him. "No treasure is worth all these lives."

"Don't be naïve, Doctor Connor. Of course it is."

"How much are we talking about?"

"At least a hundred tons of gold, probably more. It was meant to pay the armies in Korea, in the days when we had vision and courage."

"Even if you find it, you'll never be able to move it without being discovered."

"I am an influential man," Nobuyasu said. "Bribing officials is an ancient tradition in my country. I have no doubt I will recover it with only minor problems."

He looked down at Selena, impatient.

"Where is it located, Doctor Connor?"

"I can't tell yet. Somewhere near the Castle."

As she spoke, Selena entered a command that sent everything she'd been working on to Freddie. Elizabeth now had a complete copy of the document text in its original form, plus Selena's notes.

"I think you are stalling. You are running out of time." He turned to one of his men standing nearby. "Hachiro, there's something I must do. Watch her. If she gives you any trouble, break her arm."

Hachiro weighed at least three hundred pounds. Selena had seen men like him before. The weight was mostly muscle, little was fat. He moved in a way that told her he had martial arts training. It would be difficult to surprise him, but not impossible. She contemplated how to attack him.

"I know what you are thinking," Nobuyasu said. "Don't imagine you can win against him. Hachiro is exceptionally talented and very fast. He doesn't like foreigners and he doesn't like you. He'll break your arm and possibly something else if you make any wrong moves."

Selena looked at Hachiro. He began smiling at her. It wasn't a pleasant smile.

"When I return, I want the translation," Nobuyasu said. "Don't disappoint me."

He left the room.

FORTY-THREE

Nick had gone to PSIA headquarters on the other side of the city. He was sitting in Yamamoto's office when the phone rang.

Yamamoto answered, listened, and put down his phone. He turned to Nick.

"That was Director Hood. Nobuyasu is holding Doctor Connor at a house on the outskirts of the city."

"That's good work, Yamamoto-san."

"Your wife is very resourceful. She managed to send a message back to your Director Harker with her location."

"What happens next?"

"I am sending a special tactics squad to the house."

"A SWAT team? I want to be with them."

"There is no purpose in that, Nick-san. There is nothing you can do. My men are well trained. You must leave it to us."

"You expect me to sit here while you send a strike team against the house?"

"I am going there to supervise. You can ride with me."

"You're going? You surprise me."

A flash of anger crossed Yamamoto's face.

"I will excuse your rudeness, Nick. Nobuyasu is too important. If something goes wrong tonight, there will be serious repercussions. It is my duty to be there."

Nick would never understand the Japanese mind, but he understood dedication to duty.

"I meant no offense, Yamamoto-san. In America it would be impossible for the head of our CIA to accompany a strike team on a mission."

Yamamoto nodded, mollified. He picked up his phone again and issued a stream of orders in Japanese.

"Come with me."

Nick followed Yamamoto to a private elevator. They descended swiftly to the lowest level. The doors opened onto an underground parking garage where Yamamoto's car and driver were already waiting. The driver bowed and held the rear door open.

They climbed in. Yamamoto gave him instructions. The car headed up toward street level and waited. A moment later, three unmarked blue vans rolled by. When they had passed, Yamamoto's driver pulled in behind.

The target house where Nobuyasu was holding Selena was miles away, on the northern outskirts of the city.

"What's the plan?" Nick asked.

They had entered one of the expressways that funneled traffic through and around the city and were making good time.

"We surround the house and give him a chance to surrender peacefully," Yamamoto said.

"Why not surprise him?"

"Because he is Atagi Nobuyasu. I must give him the chance."

"What if he decides to fight?"

"Then I send in the teams."

"Do they know about Selena?"

"They do. It's a hostage situation. They practice for this all the time."

Nick spent the rest of the ride in silence. As far as he was concerned, warning Nobuyasu by giving him a chance to surrender was a big mistake. From what he'd seen, the man didn't strike him as the surrendering type. He thought about how things could go wrong in an operation like this. He knew what it was like. Something always went wrong, even with the best of planning.

He was worried about Selena, if she was all right. If she'd gotten a message to Harker, she must have access to a computer. Why was Nobuyasu letting her use a computer? Why had he taken her in the first place? And why was Yamamoto so concerned about Nobuyasu?

They'd been driving for an hour. Now the convoy slowed.

"We're getting close now," Yamamoto said.

He spoke into a handheld radio, then listened to the response.

"The house is surrounded by a wall. The teams will split up. If Nobuyasu does not cooperate, one team will breach the main entrance while the others come over the walls."

"Great," Nick said.

"You do not approve?"

"Would it make any difference if I didn't?"

"No."

"Then I guess I'd better hope your plan works."

FORTY-FOUR

Inside Nobuyasu's compound, Selena studied the ancient Japanese characters on her computer screen. She had substituted and rearranged them until they'd started to make sense. Once she'd discovered that the document was about something hidden near the castle in Osaka, she had been able to decrypt most of the rest. With a tap of a key, she sent what she'd translated to Virginia.

She could feel the hulking presence of Hachiro looming nearby. He smelled of cigarettes and fish and sweat, an unpleasant odor that hung in the cloud about him. She thought about how she could attack him.

Sitting on a cushion on the floor in front of the computer put her at a disadvantage. If he were closer, she might be able to pivot and attack with a kick, but he was out of range. In any event, an attack like that had no guarantee of success against someone as big and strong as he was. She'd have to gain her feet to have a fighting chance. Before she could get into position, Hachiro would take her down.

From the corner of her eye, she contemplated the sword, lying on a low table on the other side of the room. If she could get to the sword, Hachiro and the others would be history.

She remembered a teaching from Sun Tzu, about patience when faced with adversity.

If you wait by the banks of the river long enough, the bodies of your enemies will float by.

Very well, she would be patient. An opportunity would present itself, sooner or later.

Nobuyasu came into the room, accompanied by Genki.

"Time is up, Doctor Connor. What have you got?"

"I've translated most of the document."

"Good. Now, what does it say?"

"The treasure is hidden in a tunnel, not far from the castle."

"There have always been rumors it was hidden in a tunnel. Many people have looked for it. You had better not to be making this up."

"I'm not making it up. The entrance to the tunnel is under a shrine built by Hideyoshi. Directions to the shrine are given in relationship to the northeast corner of the castle. There's another section I haven't translated yet. It has to do with something in the tunnel."

"Where…"

Whatever Nobuyasu was about to say was interrupted by a blaring voice coming over a bullhorn. Selena automatically translated the words.

"Atagi Nobuyasu. This is the Public Security Agency. You are surrounded. This is your only opportunity to surrender. Please to exit the house with hands above your head. If you do not comply, we will enter by force."

Nobuyasu looked at Selena.

"You found a way to bring them here, didn't you?"

"No, I..."

He strode forward and punched her as hard as he could in the face. She crumpled to the floor, unconscious.

"Genki. Pick her up and carry her. Hachiro, grab the computer. Come with me."

Nobuyasu had come to this particular house for a reason. He picked up the Masamune sword and went into the garden. Genki and Hachiro followed, Selena limp in Genki's arms. They crossed a small bridge over a stream feeding a koi pond dotted with water lilies. On the other side of the stream was a large stone lantern, set in a bed of white pebbles.

Nobuyasu felt under the edge of the lantern and pressed a switch. The lantern rotated to the right, revealing an opening and a ladder. Genki climbed down the ladder. Hachiro handed Selena down to him, then followed. Nobuyasu went last. At the bottom of the ladder, he pressed another switch and the lantern moved back over the opening. A row of lights on the ceiling came on, illuminating a square passage paved with flat stone.

Ten minutes later, the group emerged in an underground garage. Selena was still unconscious. They walked over to a white van and got in. Hachiro got in the back with Selena. Genki got behind the wheel and started the van. Nobuyasu sat next to him.

They went up the exit ramp to the street above and turned right.

After a while, the lights of Tokyo were a distant reflection behind them.

*****

Yamamoto stood outside the house, talking to his team leader. Then he came over to where Nick stood.

"The house is empty."

"Empty? It can't be empty. Selena sent the coordinates. It has to be the right house."

"It may be the right house, however, there is no one inside."

"You waited fifteen minutes to go in after you warned him. He must've had some way to escape."

"My men were watching. He could not have escaped. If he was in the house with your wife, he left before we arrived. Do not press me, American. Remember, you are only here as a courtesy to my counterpart in your country."

Nick controlled an urge to tell Yamamoto what he could do with his courtesy.

"There is nothing more we can do here. I'll have one of my men give you a ride back to your hotel."

Yamamoto turned his back on Nick and went over to one of his men.

I'm done with this guy, Nick thought.

FORTY-FIVE

Freddie hacked into Yamamoto's server and accessed the files about Nobuyasu. Elizabeth and Stephanie were looking through them when Freddie announced the arrival of Selena's message.

I have received another message from Selena. Would you like to hear what it says?

Stephanie sighed in exasperation.

Elizabeth said, "Yes, Freddie, please tell us what it says."

The message is a translation of the document that was concealed within the hilt of the Masamune sword. It contains directions to a buried treasure hidden by Toyotomi Hideyoshi near the end of his life.

"A buried treasure?"

That is correct.

"What kind of treasure?"

The treasure is famous in Japanese history. It is referred to as the Tenshou Ooban. It is said to consist of approximately one hundred tons of gold and other valuable artifacts.

Stephanie whistled.

"One hundred tons of gold. I guess we know why Atagi was so interested in getting his hands on that sword."

Stephanie, why did you make that noise?

"It's a human thing, Freddie. A nonverbal comment of surprise at the size of the treasure."

"I wonder what a hundred tons of gold is worth?" Elizabeth asked.

One hundred tons of gold is worth approximately eleven billion six hundred and thirty-nine thousand three hundred and seventy-six dollars according to today's current spot value.

"Where did all that gold come from?" Stephanie said.

The gold was payroll for Japanese armies fighting in Korea.

"And Toyotomi Hideyoshi?"

Toyotomi Hideyoshi was the most powerful man in Japan at that time. He is the one who built Osaka Castle.

"You said the document contained directions to the treasure. Did Selena send those directions in her message?"

Affirmative.

"Freddie, can you post the translation on the monitor?"

Affirmative.

The two women looked at Selena's notes and the directions to the long-lost treasure.

"It says it's at the end of a tunnel, somewhere near Osaka Castle."

"These directions refer to landmarks of the time," Elizabeth said. "A lot has changed since then. Osaka Castle is in the middle of the city. That gold could be under hundreds of tons of concrete and steel."

It is not under tons of concrete and steel.

"It's not?"

The entrance to the tunnel is under a wooden shrine in Osaka that existed during the time of Toyotomi Hideyoshi.

"How do you know that?"

I compared the directions as written in archaic Japanese and translated by Selena with satellite photographs of the area. The entrance to the tunnel is under the sanctuary of the shrine.

"Unbelievable," Stephanie said. "A hundred tons of gold, right under everyone's nose."

That is not possible, Stephanie.

"Never mind, Freddie. It's just an expression."

Elizabeth called Nick. He told her about the raid on the house and Nobuyasu's disappearance. She briefed him on what Selena had discovered.

"Buried treasure?" Nick said. "That's what this is all about?"

"It goes back to the sword," Elizabeth said. "There was a document hidden in the hilt with directions to the location of the treasure. That's why Nobuyasu wanted the sword. He took Selena because he needed someone to translate it."

"That explains a lot."

"Selena sent Freddie a translation of the document. The gold is under a shrine near Osaka Castle."

Nick's voice was strained.

"If Selena's given him what he wanted, they don't have any more use for her."

"Not necessarily. If you didn't find her during the raid, they still need her for something. We don't know everything yet."

"Yamamoto held off going into the house long enough for Nobuyasu to get away. I think he's crooked. Maybe Nobuyasu has something on him."

"Freddie hacked into Yamamoto's files. We were starting to work on them when we got Selena's message. If there's something there, we'll find it."

"What about a weapon?"

"I'm sorry, Nick. Hood wouldn't cooperate. You'll have to improvise."

Elizabeth heard him curse over the phone.

"All right. They're going to go after the gold. If it's in Osaka, Selena will be with them. What's the quickest way to get to Osaka?"

The quickest way between Tokyo and Osaka is the Nozomi bullet train. It will take you from Tokyo to Osaka station in two hours and thirty minutes. If you need translation capabilities, use your phone and I will help you.

"Thanks, Freddie."

"What's your plan, Nick?" Elizabeth asked.

"I'm going after her. I don't give a damn how important Nobuyasu is supposed to be, he's going down."

"You need to be careful. If you kill him, I can't protect you."

"I'll try not to. But if he's hurt Selena…"

He left the sentence unfinished.

FORTY-SIX

Selena was in pain. Her hands were bound together in front of her. She touched her face and winced. Gingerly, she moved her jaw. It hurt, but she didn't think it was broken.

I wouldn't have believed that little bastard could punch that hard.

She lay on the carpeted floor of an empty room. There were no windows. She didn't know where she was, but she had a sense of being in a large building. Maybe an apartment somewhere. She thought she heard the faint hum of a city, more vibration than sound.

She got to her knees, then her feet. There were two doors in the room. One led to an empty closet. The other to whatever lay outside the room.

Gently, she tried the handle of the door. It was locked.

There was nothing in the room she could use as a weapon. With her hands tied, she was at a disadvantage.

How long had she been here? How long unconscious? There was no way to tell. Her message about the location in Osaka would have reached Elizabeth. She would have passed it on to Nick. It was only a question of time before he came after her. It didn't take a rocket scientist to figure out Nobuyasu would be headed for the spot where the gold was hidden. Her best hope was that Nick would get there ahead of him.

It occurred to her that she was alive because part of the document hadn't been translated. Once Nobuyasu decided there was nothing more to learn from her, he'd kill her. He'd only keep her alive as long as she was of some benefit to him.

She heard the lock on the door click. She stepped away, ready for whatever came next.

The door opened. Hachiro stood in a hallway outside the room, glowering at her.

"You. Come. No trouble or I hurt you."

He stepped aside as she came out of the room and pushed her to the left, down the hall. She passed a closed door on her right. The hallway ended in a large living room with a picture window looking out over a city. From the quality of the light, she guessed it was midday. She'd been unconscious for many hours.

Nobuyasu sat on a Western-style couch under the window. He watched her with eyes that reminded her of a black mamba, a poisonous snake she'd seen in Africa.

"You have caused problems, Doctor Connor," he said. "It would have been simpler if you had cooperated. But it doesn't matter. It's time for you to continue your task. Finish the translation."

"Why should I? You're only going to kill me at the end of it. Don't deny it, I can see it in your eyes."

"Not necessarily. If you cooperate now, I will think about letting you live."

"And if I don't?"

"You are probably not aware of the many ways in which my ancestors treated those whom they regarded as enemies or spies. Please believe me when I tell you that if you don't do as I ask, you will think your fires of hell a field of bliss compared to what I will do to you."

"You would resort to torture?"

"I prefer to think of it as scientific persuasion. Come now, Doctor Connor, we are both civilized people. There's no need for such nastiness. Finish the translation. I assure you, I will be grateful. Or would you prefer that I allow Hachiro to do what he likes with you before I begin questioning you in earnest?"

"You are a despicable human being," Selena said.

"Names will not affect me. Time to decide, Doctor Connor. What do you say? Will you finish the translation?"

His eyes told her he wasn't bluffing.

"You leave me no choice."

"There's always a choice. In this case, you've made the right one. The computer is over there on that table. For your information, it is no longer connected to the Internet. Don't think you can send something to your friends."

He was watching her carefully as he spoke. He must've seen something in her eyes.

"Ah, as I thought. That's what brought the security agency to my door. Well, that's not going to happen again. You have enough information to finish. Perhaps you should get started."

"I need my hands untied."

"Hachiro," Nobuyasu said.

Hachiro came forward, took out a knife and cut the bonds around her wrists. She rubbed her hands.

"Begin, Doctor Connor. Time is fleeting."

She sat down at the table and opened the file with the partially completed translation.

FORTY-SEVEN

Nick took a taxi from the hotel to the train station. There were many trains leaving each hour. The next train for Osaka was the *Nozomi*, the one Freddie had recommended. Nick bought a ticket and waited behind a steel barrier on the platform.

The train was only moderately crowded, unusual for any kind of public transportation in Japan. Once on board, he took a comfortable seat by a window. An electronic display at the end of the car scrolled a steady stream of Japanese characters.

Soon the train was speeding across the Japanese landscape at almost two hundred miles an hour. Half an hour after he boarded, an attendant came through the train with a food trolley. Nick couldn't remember when he'd last eaten. He bought a box of food covered with Japanese characters he couldn't read. It had a picture of a samurai on it. The box contained an assortment of fish and rice wrapped in seaweed.

It wasn't bad, but the food didn't do anything to relieve his fears for Selena.

He closed his eyes and tried to get a feeling for where she was, what she was doing, if she was still alive. Try as he might, he could get no sense of her. Nobuyasu was a loose cannon. Nick was certain he'd kill her, once he'd gotten what he wanted from her.

He didn't know what he'd do if he lost her, except for one thing. If she died, he would not rest until Nobuyasu was dead.

He wished Ronnie and Lamont were with him, but there wasn't time to wait for them to get here. He wished he had a weapon. It would take time to find something, and time was something he didn't have.

For the rest of the trip his mind whirled with images of mayhem and revenge.

At Shin-Osaka station, he pulled out his phone and called Virginia. Elizabeth answered.

"I'm in Osaka. I need Freddie to help me get to this shrine."

"Hold on," she said.

Freddie came on line.

I will be happy to help you, Nick. Did you have an enjoyable train ride? I have wondered what it would be like to ride on a train.

Nick restrained himself from shouting.

"It was fast. Freddie, I'm going out to the taxi rank. I need you to tell the driver where I have to go."

Affirmative.

"Stay on the line."

Affirmative.

It was humid and warm in Osaka, the sky heavy with ominous looking clouds lit by streaks of lightning in the distance.

There were many taxis to choose from. All of them showed a red light in the passenger side window. Nick chose a medium-size Toyota. As he approached the car and reached for the door, it opened automatically. He got in.

"Do you speak English?" he asked the driver.

The man shook his head. "No English."

"Okay. Freddie, tell this guy where I'm going."

He held up his phone and listened to a stream of Japanese as Freddie told the driver where Nick wanted to go. If the taxi driver was surprised by being given directions over a phone, he didn't show it.

The driver said something. Freddie translated.

He says that the shrine will be closed at night.

"Tell him to let me off near the entrance to the shrine anyway."

The driver listened to Freddie's voice over the phone, shrugged, set the meter, and pulled away from the station.

FORTY-EIGHT

Daylight had come and gone. Selena had been stymied for hours with the last part of the translation, when suddenly the meaning of the coded words fell into place. It gave her hope. Maybe there would be a way out of this.

She looked up from the computer and stretched.

"Well?" Nobuyasu said.

"I've got it, but you may not like it."

"Don't play games, Doctor Connor. What have you found?"

"The entrance to the tunnel is under the sanctuary in the shrine. According to this, it's directly under the altar where the representation of the *kami* is placed. But there's a problem."

"What problem?"

"Assuming the tunnel still exists, the document says a barrier has been placed before the treasure can be reached."

"What kind of barrier?"

"A puzzle. The characters are a very old form of the word for gate or passage. That's one of the things that was giving me trouble. The puzzle must be solved before anyone can pass through the gate to the place where the treasure is kept."

Selena saw no need to tell Nobuyasu that the passage about the tunnel, the puzzle, and the gate warned of danger.

"That's it? It doesn't give any more information about this puzzle?"

"No."

"She's finished what you asked her to do," Hachiro said.

There was anticipation in his voice. Selena heard it.

"You need to take me along," Selena said.

"Why should I do that, Doctor Connor? The translation is complete."

"What if the puzzle requires you to solve a riddle or an instruction? It will be written in the same kind of code as the document. You won't be able to understand it. If you can't understand it, you won't reach the gold. You need to take me along."

"She is playing games," Hachiro said.

Nobuyasu gave Selena a hard look. She stared back, unflinching.

"Perhaps," he said, "but we can't take the chance. She may still be useful. Take her back to her room and lock her in."

Selena got up and walked ahead of Hachiro back to the room.

"You are planning something," Hachiro said. "Whatever it is, it's not going to work."

He pushed her into the room, grinned, and gripped his crotch. "I'm going to make you beg me to stop."

He closed the door.

Asshole.

She waited. After some time, she fell asleep, waking when the door opened again. Nobuyasu stood there with Genki and Hachiro.

"It's time. The lives of your children depend on your cooperation. You understand?"

"Yes."

Nobuyasu led the way. Selena was sandwiched between Genki and Hachiro. Hachiro kept one huge hand on her neck all the time. She wanted to rip it away and gouge out his eyes, but this wasn't the place or time. They got into an elevator and descended to an underground parking garage, then walked to a white Honda work van. There were no windows in the back. It was the kind of vehicle seen everywhere in Japan. Hachiro opened the back doors, pushed Selena inside, then climbed in after her.

The shrine was located a short distance away from the towering castle that was Osaka's main tourist attraction. The original castle had been home to the shoguns who ruled Japan during the feudal period. It had burned down in the nineteenth century, then been partly rebuilt and used as an arsenal during World War II. It had been rebuilt again in the 90s. It was now one of Japan's major historical monuments.

It was past midnight. The streets near the shrine were deserted.

"Park over there," Nobuyasu said.

Genki pulled the van into a narrow street leading to the shrine and parked. They got out of the car. Nobuyasu carried the Masamune sword, unwilling to let it out of his sight. Genki and Hachiro carried flashlights.

Nobuyasu held the sword up in front of her. "Remember, no trouble."

At the end of the street was a set of ancient steps leading to the entrance of the shrine. Columns inscribed with Japanese characters lined both sides of the steps as they climbed.

At the top of the steps was a wooden fence and a gate painted red. A narrow path led a short distance to a second gate and the shrine itself, an ancient building of wood with a curving roof that had somehow survived the bombs of World War II.

She looked around. The grounds were landscaped in the way only the Japanese seemed able to achieve, large shrubs and trees and flowers placed to create a sense of harmony and peace. Selena had seen no one since they left the van, yet it felt like someone was watching. She thought she saw movement behind one of the shrubs.

Her heart begin thumping.

Nick? Could it be him?

Hachiro placed his hand on the back of her neck again. It wasn't a pleasant grip. She could feel his strength. It would be easy for him to crush her throat.

Two stone lion-dogs guarded the entrance, one with its mouth wide open, the other closed. They passed between them and entered a room where visitors worshiped. Nobuyasu led them past that to a hall where offerings were left.

"Where is the sanctuary?" Selena asked.

"You're looking at it," Nobuyasu said.

Straight ahead was a raised section of floor and two closed wooden doors. Nobuyasu pulled the doors open. Inside was a small room with a mirror on the back wall. The floor was covered with tatami mats.

"Genki, pull away the mats."

Underneath the mats was a wooden floor, turned dark with time. There was nothing to indicate the entrance to a tunnel.

"There has to be a hidden catch," Selena said. "A lot of temples and shrines in this period had concealed passages."

"Maybe there's nothing here. Maybe she's been misleading us," Genki said.

"That would be unfortunate. But I don't think she'd risk her children. Would you, Doctor Connor?"

"You know I wouldn't."

"Then find the entrance."

The walls of the sanctuary were made of the same wood as the floor. Selena allowed her eyes to wander over the room. She kept coming back to the mirror, meant to represent the spirit of the shrine. The frame was old, as old as the building itself. It was made of cypress. A flower was carved in the wood on top of the mirror. It was the only decoration in the room.

"What kind of flower is that?" Selena asked.

"What difference does it make?" Genki said.

"I'm thinking of your tradition of *hanakatoba*, the meaning of flowers."

"It's probably a camellia," Nobuyasu said. "That was a popular symbol during the time of Hideyoshi. It means love. But it can also mean a noble death."

"That would fit him," Selena said. "I saw something like this once in an English castle. It was a rose carved into a fireplace mantle. You pressed on it, and it opened a secret panel. That flower might be a catch to release the hidden entrance."

"Get out of the way."

Nobuyasu reached out with the sword and pushed at the center of the flower. There was a loud click. A section in the middle of the floor swung down and away, leaving a dark opening.

"Very good, Doctor Connor. Hachiro, give me your light."

Nobuyasu shone the light down into the opening. A wooden ladder descended to the floor below.

"I'm going down. Hachiro you come next. Bring her. Genki, you come last."

One by one they went down the ladder. At the bottom, the flashlights revealed a tunnel shored up with beams and posts of wood. The ceiling had been covered with planks of cypress. It reminded Selena of a mine. She hated mines. The last time she'd been in something like this, she'd been surrounded by rats and spiders.

She didn't see any spiders. The tunnel was dank and unpleasant and smelled of damp earth and decaying wood. She was surprised it was still intact after all these centuries. How it had survived the frequent earthquakes in the region was beyond her. Looking at the old beams and crumbling earth of the walls, she didn't think it would survive much longer.

They followed the tunnel, the ceiling a few inches above Selena's head. She could feel the weight of tons of earth above her. The floor was littered with rubble that had accumulated over centuries, the result of the frequent tremors in the region. It was hot. The air was thick and heavy. Selena found herself longing for clean air.

This whole thing could collapse at any time, she thought.

An involuntary shiver rippled through her body at the thought of being buried alive here, under the dark, dank earth. Buried where she would never be found, alone in the dark. She imagined the tunnel caving in, dirt and rock crushing her, blocking her nose and mouth, choking off her breath. She realized she was clenching her hands into fists. She forced herself to relax and push away the fear.

Genki had moved to the front, walking ahead of everyone else. Suddenly the floor of the tunnel gave way under his feet. He screamed and fell out of sight. His scream was cut short, trailing off into a wet gurgle.

Nobuyasu shone his light down into a deep pit filled with sharp, wooden spikes. Genki was dead, his face twisted in agony, his body impaled. One spike had pushed through his chest, another through his groin, a third through his shoulder.

Nobuyasu turned to Selena, his face dark with rage.

"You knew, didn't you?"

"No, how could I know? There was nothing about a trap, only the puzzle."

"She's lying," Hachiro said.

Nobuyasu gripped Selena tightly by the arm. She winced at the pain.

"Doctor Connor. You will go first. In case there are any more surprises."

A narrow space had been left on each side of the pit. With her back pressed against the wall of the tunnel, Selena inched across and waited on the other side. There was no point in trying to escape. There was nowhere to go.

One down. The odds just got better.

Nobuyasu crossed and pushed her forward.

"Any games, I cut off your head," Nobuyasu said.

A few minutes later, the tunnel curved to the right. They came to a wall blocking the way forward. A row of five wooden handles projected from slots in the center of the wall. Each handle had a square block on the end carved with characters.

"Now what?" Hachiro said.

"This must be the puzzle," Selena said.

"I can't read what's written there," Nobuyasu said.

"That's because the characters are in the same code as the document."

"Can you read it?"

"Yes. But I have to figure out how it works. I think the handles have to be moved in a certain order."

"And what if you get it wrong?"

"I assure you, I don't want to get it wrong. Bad things will happen if the wrong sequence is used. Look at the roof."

She pointed up at the wooden ceiling. Faint lines were visible in the wood, running across the neatly fitted planks.

"That has to be a trap. I've seen things like this before. My guess is the roof will collapse if I don't get it right. We'll all be killed."

"Not quite. Only you, Doctor Connor. If that's a trap, you will be the one standing under it."

Nobuyasu and Hachiro backed a safe distance away.

"Doctor Connor."

"What do you want, Nobuyasu?"

"You may begin."

FORTY-NINE

Selena studied the characters on the five levers projecting from the wall.

"I think these are place names," she said. "This one says Yamazaki."

"Yamazaki is in Kyoto," Nobuyasu said. "It is the site of a famous battle during the reign of Hideyoshi."

"The next one reads Anegawa."

"Another battle where Hideyoshi led troops."

She pointed to another one. "Shizugatake?"

"That is one of the greatest battles in our history. It was magnificent. Hideyoshi emerged victorious and consolidated his power."

"What about this one? Takamatsu?"

"That too is a battle where Hideyoshi was victorious, early in his career. He laid siege to a castle controlled by a rival clan."

"This last one says Odawara."

"That is the final battle Hideyoshi fought," Nobuyasu said. "After that, he established his rule and began the invasions of Korea."

"It's a pattern," Selena said. "Each one of these is a battle where Hideyoshi fought and won. The puzzle is a monument to his ego."

"Hideyoshi became a great general. All of these are from different stages in his military career," Nobuyasu said. "He was a true samurai, even though he came from common stock."

"I'm sure these levers have to be used in a correct sequence. What was the first battle he fought in, among the ones listed here?"

"Anegawa. He had not yet achieved great fame and was still known as Hashiba Hideyoshi."

The lever marked Anegawa was in the middle of the row.

"Which battle came next?"

"Takamatsu."

That lever was on the end.

"And then?"

"Then Yamazaki, Shizugutake, and Odawara, in that order."

She'd get one chance. If she didn't use those levers in the right order, she was certain the roof would collapse and kill her. What was the right combination? Should she enter the battles in the order they took place? Or should she start with Hideyoshi's last, great, success and work backwards? Or was there some other possible combination? Whatever it was, Nobuyasu was getting impatient.

"Make up your mind, Doctor Connor. We are running out of time. I want to leave here before dawn and I can always come back at a future date. Decide."

She thought about what kind of man Hideyoshi had been. An alpha male, for sure. In the culture of the time, he would've been arrogant and conceited, a man who would want people to remember his victories and successes, to admire his progression through life until he became all-powerful.

I'm Hideyoshi and I'm a product of my time, she thought. *I want people to see how I earned my high rank through courage and valor. I want them to remember how I fought my way to the top. How I defeated my enemies.*

She pulled down the lever marked with the first of Hideyoshi's victories.

Anegawa.

Something moved behind the wall. A stream of dust fell from the ceiling above her. She looked up and took a breath.

Takamatsu.

More dust.

Yamazaki. Shizugutake.

She got ready to make a run for it. Maybe she could make it to where Nobuyasu stood with Hachiro if the roof started to come down.

Odawara.

She pulled down the final lever.

FIFTY

Nick was waiting in the shadows when Nobuyasu and his goons showed up with Selena. He watched them enter the shrine and pass through the outer hall into the room beyond. Once they were inside he followed, keeping his distance.

They entered the sanctuary and disappeared. After a few moments, he followed them.

At the entrance to the tunnel, he paused, listening. He couldn't hear them. He climbed down the ladder and began to feel his way along the tunnel, trying not to make any noise. He could see nothing in the utter blackness until the glow of flashlights ahead told him where they were. Bending down, he picked up a rock the size of a baseball. It wasn't as good as a gun, but it was better than nothing.

He could see Selena and the others moving along the tunnel ahead of him. A large man had his hand wrapped around Selena's neck as they walked.

I'm going to kill him, Nick thought. *Thank God she's okay.*

His ear began tingling.

One of Nobuyasu's men walked in front of the others. Suddenly he disappeared with a scream. From his place in the darkness behind them, Nick watched the group stop and look down. Nobuyasu turned to Selena. Their voices echoed down the tunnel.

"You knew, didn't you?"

"No, how could I know? There was nothing about a trap, only the puzzle."

"She's lying."

"Doctor Connor. You will go first. In case there are any more surprises."

Nick waited until they were all on the other side of the trap and farther along the tunnel. He hurried before he lost the glow of their lights. At the edge of the pit he could made out Genki's body impaled on the spikes below. The man had been an enemy, but it was a death Nick wouldn't wish on anyone.

He crossed the ledge on the side of the pit and continued down the tunnel, until he saw they had stopped in front of the wall blocking the way.

He heard Selena say there was a trap. Nobuyasu told her she had to risk it and solve the puzzle in front of her. He heard them talking about Hideyoshi and the battles. Then Selena pulled down a lever sticking out of the wall.

Oh, shit, he thought. *What if she gets it wrong?*

One by one, she pulled the levers down. With the last one, she jumped back toward Nobuyasu. From somewhere deep underground came the sound of an ancient mechanism grinding, gears turning. The wooden wall slowly opened inward, revealing darkness.

Nobuyasu pointed his flashlight into whatever lay ahead.

"After you, Doctor Connor," he said.

"There may be more traps. It won't help if I can't see them. If you want me to go first, give me a flashlight."

Nobuyasu smiled unpleasantly and handed her his light.

"Don't think you can use it as a weapon," Nobuyasu said. He held up the sword. "If you try anything, I will cut off your arm. Believe me, you're not fast enough."

Selena stepped through the opening.

FIFTY-ONE

The first thing she saw in the beam from her flashlight were wooden boxes piled against the near wall. She moved the light. It fell on a torch set in an iron holder, mounted on the wall by the door.

"There's a torch. Do you have a lighter? Matches?"

"Hachiro. Give me your lighter."

Muttering something, Hachiro handed over the lighter. Nobuyasu passed it on to Selena. She went to the torch. It was made of wood, the end coated with a black, tarry substance.

She clicked the lighter on, reached up, and held it next to the end of the torch. It smoldered, caught, and burst into flame.

The yellowish, dancing light from the torch cast long shadows about the chamber. The room was lined with stone. She couldn't see the rear wall. Thick beams held up the ceiling. A wooden chest near the entrance stood open. The contents glittered in the light of the torch, oblong gold coins laid out in neat rows.

Hideyoshi's stolen treasure.

"Oh, boy," she said.

Nobuyasu and Hachiro came into the room. They stopped and stared.

Selena went to the wall on the left and lit another torch. She was running out of time. She had to make a move.

The torches revealed a room fifty feet long and as wide again. It was stacked with cases of gold. Aisles ran between them. There was a cleared area in the middle of the room, perhaps twenty feet to a side.

The light from the second torch revealed the far wall. A shot of adrenaline froze her in place. A horned figure stood there, like a demon placed to guard the gold. Then she realized it was a full suit of armor with a horned helmet, mounted on a stand.

At its side hung two swords. Nobuyasu saw it at the same time and knew what she would do.

"No!" he shouted. "Hachiro, get her."

Selena ran to the armor and drew out the long katana that had been the mark of the samurai. It came out of the scabbard with a deadly whisper. She could feel the blade vibrate in her hands. It looked blood red in the flickering light of the torches. In the cool darkness of the underground room, the hilt felt warm, as if it were alive.

Hachiro stopped when he saw her holding the sword.

"You still going to make me beg you to stop?" Selena said.

Hachiro backed away. Selena advanced toward him, the sword held straight up before her in both hands. Nobuyasu moved down an aisle to flank her. Hachiro sidled off to the side, aiming to circle behind her and reach the armor with its second sword. Both men were out of reach.

A dark object hurtled through the air and struck Hachiro on the side of his head.

He grunted and went down, clutching his head in both hands.

"Selena!" Nick yelled. "I'll take care of him. Get Nobuyasu."

"Took you long enough," she called out.

"He can't help you," Nobuyasu said. "When I'm done with you, I'm going to cut him in half."

"You talk a lot," she said.

"We have national competitions with the swords," Nobuyasu said. "I was All Japan Champion with the katana. You're not good enough, Doctor Connor."

Selena decided to save her breath. The voice of her teacher echoed in her mind. Over many years, Master Kim had taught her the art of the sword.

"Some opponents boast and strut about like peacocks. Never engage in their foolishness. They will try to fill your mind with doubt. Ignore their words. Center your Chi. Pull the energy from the earth, up through your feet, your body, your arms, until it is at the very tip of your weapon, until you and the weapon are one."

"And then?"

"And then, you will be invincible."

Her focus was on Nobuyasu, but from the corner of her eye she saw Hachiro rise to his feet. Blood streamed down the side of his face. Nick was moving toward him.

"What do you say, Doctor Connor?" Nobuyasu called. "Let's meet in the middle.

There's plenty of room. Let's see how good you are."

For a second she thought about it. It wouldn't be easy to maneuver in the narrow aisles between the boxes of gold. She'd have a better shot with space around her. In a confined space, she'd be at a disadvantage.

"All right," she called.

Nobuyasu laughed, a sound bordering on madness, fueled by adrenaline and the warped conceits that made him who he was.

They came into the square in the middle of the room from opposite sides, swords ready. Selena heard the sounds of Nick and Hachiro fighting. Then she shut everything out except her opponent.

FIFTY-TWO

Hachiro had gotten to his feet. Nick charged him with a running tackle, knocking him down. Hachiro rolled to the side and leapt back up. Nick backed away. Hachiro gave him an evil look and grinned.

"Now I will kill you," he said.

"You know what, asshole? You stink. You smell like rotten fish."

Hachiro's face turned dark and he charged. Nick twisted to the side and landed a hard kick. He'd aimed for the knee, but hit the thigh instead. It was like kicking a wall. Hachiro slammed his fist into Nick's chest. It felt like he'd been shot. Sharp pain radiated down his side.

He didn't have time to think about it before Hachiro hit him again in the same spot. Pain shot through his chest. Something broke. Hachiro threw another punch. Nick ducked under and kicked him in the groin.

There was no better way to bring down an opponent, no matter how big, but Hachiro didn't go down. He grunted and stood there, momentarily stunned by the shock. It was the split-second Nick needed. He launched another kick, this time connecting with a knee. It broke with a loud snap. Hachiro's leg bent backward at an impossible angle and he went to the floor. Nick tried to kick him in the head. The big Japanese grabbed his leg and pulled it out from under him.

Nick landed on his back as Hachiro tried to rise. Nick kicked again with his free leg and caught Hachiro under the chin, snapping his head back. Hachiro let go. Nick got to his feet and jumped into the air, landing with both feet and all his two hundred pounds on Hachiro's chest.

The bones snapped with a harsh, ugly sound. Hachiro's eyes went wide and rolled back into his head. He took two rasping breaths. Blood shot from his mouth. Then he stopped breathing.

Nick's chest felt like it was on fire.

Selena.

In the center of the chamber, Selena and Nobuyasu faced each other.

"This should be interesting," Nobuyasu said. "Shall we observe the formalities?"

"I don't think so," Selena said.

"Pity. Come, Doctor Connor, let's see how good you really are."

He gave off a loud yell and attacked with a horizontal strike, but Selena was ready for him. She parried the thrust and countered. The blades rang together, a bell-like sound that echoed through the room.

"You have a good blade," Nobuyasu said. "I will add it to my collection."

He tried an overhead strike. Selena parried and moved, but the Masamune sword grazed her left arm. The blade was so sharp that she barely felt it. Blood bloomed on her blouse.

"First blood, Doctor Connor."

Nobuyasu was as good as he'd said he was. For an instant she thought she might

not win. Master Kim had prepared her for
that thought.

*One day you will face an opponent
better than you. There is always someone
better, always someone who has the
potential to defeat you. If the contest is one
of life or death, doubt may creep in while
you are engaged. You must push such
thoughts away or you will surely lose. Trust
your abilities, your skill. Even the best
opponent will eventually present an opening.
Then you will strike.*

It was great advice, except that
Nobuyasu had given her no opening.

She could feel herself starting to
weaken. The katana was a two-handed
weapon. She was running out of time before
the loss of blood would leave her weak,
vulnerable to one of his strikes.

Nobuyasu backed away a step.

"You're bleeding quite a bit, Doctor
Connor. Soon you will lose strength in your
arm. Your sword will drop. All I have to do
is wait. I haven't decided if I want to take
your head or simply cut you in half."

Selena tuned out his words. She
focused, pulling up energy from the earth as
Master Kim had instructed. She felt the Chi
moving through her.

She entered the zone.

She attacked. Nobuyasu seemed to
move as if he were underwater. He brought
his blade around in a sweeping arc to cut her

in half. She parried and thrust the point of her sword deep into his abdomen.

He froze. She pulled out the sword. Normal time returned.

Nobuyasu clutched his abdomen with his left hand, looking down at the blood oozing through his fingers. He raised his eyes, took his hand away, and raised his sword. His face was tight with pain.

"Don't," she said. "You could still live. We'll get you to a doctor."

"I recognize your sword," he said, forcing the words out. "By the look of the blade, it is a Muramasa. It is the only sword that could match a Masamune."

"Put your sword down."

Nobuyasu smiled. "You know I can't do that."

He attacked. Selena parried, swung her sword, and took off his head. The body swayed and toppled to the floor, pumping blood. The head rolled away and came to rest against a chest of gold.

She looked down at the body and lowered her sword. Then Nick was at her side.

"Selena."

"I feel dizzy," she said.

"Give me the sword."

She handed it to him. He laid it on the ground and helped her sit on one of the chests.

"I'll stop the bleeding."

He tore a strip from his shirt and made a makeshift bandage.

"It's deep, but you're lucky. He missed the artery."

"He was good, the best I've ever faced. I thought I was going to lose."

"But you didn't. Are you still dizzy?"

"No, I'm all right now."

"Can you walk?"

She nodded. He helped her stand and gasped at sudden pain in his side.

"Nick. You're hurt."

"I'll be all right. Might have broken a rib. That ape hit me pretty hard."

"He was a horrible man," Selena said.

"I saw him with his hand on your neck and I wanted to kill him."

"You did."

"Let's get out of here."

"We should take the swords."

"To hell with the swords. Someone can come get them later."

He helped her stand. He picked up Nobuyasu's flashlight. They began the walk back to the shrine. They came to the death pit and he helped her across.

That was when the ground moved under their feet.

FIFTY-THREE

"Did you feel that?" Nick said.

"It was a tremor."

"I've got a bad feeling about this."

The earth shook again. They staggered to keep their balance. Dirt sifted down between the seams of the cypress planks lining the roof of the tunnel.

"Run," Nick said.

They ran down the tunnel. Every step sent agonizing shocks through Nick's side. Another tremor almost knocked them to their feet. Planks were starting to come down from the ceiling.

The walls of the tunnel were moving. Dirt poured from the ceiling. A low, rumbling vibration began.

The ladder to the shrine was ahead. The sound of the earthquake echoed through the tunnel, like the roar of a primeval beast.

They reached the ladder.

"Go," Nick yelled.

Selena started up the rungs. Behind them the roof of the tunnel was coming down, a cascade of dirt and noise and rock.

Nick grasped the ladder and started up, his ribs protesting with sharp stabs of pain. Selena got to the top, reached down with her good arm, and helped pull him out of the hole.

The floor tilted under their feet. They scrambled through the shrine and out into the open, out of the building. Something fell behind them with a loud crash.

The earth shook and groaned, knocking them off their feet. A crack opened in the ground, widening as they watched. The noise was deafening. Nick tried to stand, but the shaking earth made it impossible.

The crack grew wider, moving toward them. He grabbed Selena's hand.

"Come on."

They crawled as fast as they could on hands and knees, trying to get away from the gap racing toward them. It caught up to them and Selena slipped over the edge. Nick had her hand. He grabbed her arm with his other hand.

"Nick."

She looked up at him, terrified.

"Hold on. I've got you. Hold on."

Slowly, he pulled her back from the edge, his chest on fire. The chasm in the earth started to close. Desperate, Nick pulled with all his strength and got her out. Seconds later, the walls of the crack slammed together.

The rumbling and vibration died away. They lay on the ground, exhausted.

"Is it over?"

"I think so," Nick said. "For now. There may be aftershocks."

Sirens wailed in the city outside the grounds of the shrine. A glow lit the sky in the distance. Something was on fire.

"That was close," Nick said.

"Too close."

They stood. Nick hugged her, then took out his phone. Harker picked up.

"Yes, Nick."

"Nobuyasu is dead. We found the treasure. It's buried for good, along with Nobuyasu and his thugs."

"I told you not to kill him," Elizabeth said.

"I didn't, Selena did. It was him or us. I don't think you have to worry. No one is going to find his body anytime soon, if ever."

Nick heard Elizabeth sigh over the phone.

"I'll call you later. We both need to get to a hospital."

"All right, Nick. Call me when you can."

FIFTY-FOUR

The earthquake had done a lot of damage. Train service was disrupted, electricity cut off. Some main highways were impassable. New buildings in Osaka were constructed to withstand much larger quakes with minor damage. Older structures like the shrine didn't fare well.

Nick and Selena made their way to a hospital. Nick had two broken ribs. A doctor patched up Selena's arm. He asked her what had happened.

"This looks like a cut from a knife," he said.

"Part of a storm gutter came off a building and cut me. It was metal and very sharp. I was lucky it didn't hit me on the neck."

"You are lucky it didn't sever the brachial artery," the doctor said. "You would not have survived, even with the temporary bandage you had when you came in."

If you only knew, she thought.

They left the hospital and found a hotel.

In the room, Nick said, "With the trains off-line, we'll take a plane back to Tokyo. We'll get home as soon as we can."

"I'm going to call Anna," Selena said.

Nick went to take a shower. When he came out, Selena was off the phone.

"How are the kids?"

"Both of them are fine," she said. "It's been difficult for Anna. I think she's having trouble adjusting to the fact that she killed someone. Anyway, Jason has a new tooth and he's been crying a lot."

"They'll be teething for months. I'm more worried about any damage from what happened in the loft."

"Anna says they seem fine, but that both of them startle easily when they hear a noise."

"That figures," Nick said. "They'll get over it, with time and plenty of attention. What's good is they hear noises that startle them. With all that gunfire, I was worried about their hearing."

"How did this happen, Nick?"

"What do you mean?"

"I thought we were done with this kind of violence."

"So did I."

"I think we need to reconsider what we're doing. Working with Elizabeth and all that."

"There'll be time to think about it. When Atagi hired us to find the sword, it seemed pretty straightforward. There wasn't any reason to anticipate what happened. How could anyone know the sword held the key to all that gold?"

"But that's what always happens," Selena said. "It was different when we were working for the Project. We knew what we might be getting into. We trained for it. We had weapons and backing. We knew we were doing something to protect the country. It was a risk we took on willingly."

She paused. Nick waited.

"Now, we're consultants. Consultants are supposed to consult. They're not supposed to get involved in things like what just happened."

"You have a point."

"Nobuyasu told me he'd kill you if I didn't cooperate. Then he got around to threatening Jason and Katrina. I'm sure he was going to kill me after I finished translating that document. The only reason I'm still here is that he needed me in to figure out a puzzle mentioned in the directions to the treasure."

"That was the wall where you pulled down those handles?"

"That's right."

"What about the pit with the spikes? Did you know about that?"

"No, but the translation warned about danger in the tunnel. I didn't tell him that. Then we came to that wall. If I'd moved those levers in the wrong sequence, the roof would've come down. I'd be dead."

"But you aren't."

"I'm not putting myself in that kind of situation again. I don't mind helping Elizabeth. But I'm not going out in the field again."

"This wasn't supposed to be the field. It was about translating Japanese. That's why you came."

"I know. After everything else that had happened, we knew we might run into trouble. It's my own fault. From now on I'm staying home with our children."

Nick's phone indicated a call.

"It's Harker."

Selena sighed. "You'd better take it."

"Yes, Director," Nick answered.

"We've been looking at the files Yamamoto didn't want you to see concerning Nobuyasu."

"He's dead," Nick said. "What does it matter now?"

"Nobuyasu was partnered with the yakuza in their heroin business. Yamamoto was protecting him."

"I knew it," Nick said. "I knew something wasn't right."

"Nobuyasu was blackmailing Yamamoto. I don't know what he had on him. Whatever it was, it was enough to stop Yamamoto from looking too closely into what Nobuyasu was doing. If it ever got out that Yamamoto was giving that kind of protection to someone, he'd be fired and imprisoned. In Japan, his humiliation would be public. He'd be disgraced. Ruined."

"What are we going to do about it?" Nick asked.

"We're not going to do anything."

"Director, you just got finished telling me the head of Japan's CIA turned a blind eye to drug trafficking. We have to do something."

"This isn't the time to ride in on a white horse, Nick. Things are unstable in Japan. A scandal of this nature will bring down the government. We can't give the militarists a chance to take power. The last time they were in charge, we got World War II."

"So once again, political considerations take precedence over what's right."

"It's the way the world is," Elizabeth said. "I don't like it anymore than you do."

"He needs to be held to account."

"Stay away from Yamamoto, Nick. That's an order."

"You know what, Director? I'm tired of thinking about this. Selena and I are going to take it easy this afternoon and have a nice dinner in the restaurant downstairs later on. We'll talk when I get back."

He hung up.

"Nick? Did you hang up on her?"

He told her what she'd said.

"It's always the same old bullshit," he said. "You can't go after some people because they're too damn important. I didn't expect to hear it from Harker."

"We couldn't do much about Yamamoto, even if we wanted to."

"Maybe not. It rubs me the wrong way, that's all."

In the room next to Nick and Selena, two Japanese men were recording the conversation.

"He's not going to like this," one of them said.

FIFTY-FIVE

Yamamoto listened to the recording. Genzo and Futoshi, the men who had brought it to him, waited patiently. They were in Yamamoto's home, away from the hidden microphones and surveillance at agency headquarters.

Yamamoto looked at his two henchmen.

"How unfortunate. I rather liked them. They have displayed true courage."

"What do you want us to do?" Genzo said.

"They will have to be eliminated."

"They've booked a flight to America tomorrow."

"Then you'll have to do it tonight. Make it look as though the yakuza did it."

"That shouldn't be hard to do," Futoshi said.

"Inform me when it's done."

The two men bowed in unison. They left the house and got in their car.

Genzo said, "Looks like the boss stepped in it, big time."

"All the big shots are like that," Futoshi said. "Show me a politician who doesn't have secrets."

Genzo was driving. He pulled away from the house and headed for the expressway.

"How do you want to do this?" he said.

"Everyone has been trying to kill these Americans. No one has succeeded. I don't think we should go after them one-on-one."

"You have a better idea?"

"Maybe a bomb. We put it in their hotel room."

"Boss said make it look like the yakuza are responsible. They don't usually do bombs. Besides, where do we get one?"

"We'll improvise. The components are easy enough to find. We'll do a little shopping, make up a nice package, and deliver it."

"I don't like it. It's too complicated," Genzo said.

"Okay, smart ass, how do you want to do it?"

"We shoot them. Maybe a lot of other people with them. Make it look like a yakuza hit."

Futoshi laughed.

"You crazy bastard."

"We know where they're going to be. In the hotel restaurant. We could get them there."

"I saw a movie once where someone put a bomb in a serving cart and took it into a restaurant."

"You're still thinking about a bomb?"

"A tablecloth hid the bottom of the cart. No one suspected the bomb was underneath."

"It must have been an American movie," Genzo said.

"It was, but American movies are inferior. Ours are much better at presenting violence. The Americans are always blowing things up. It's easy and it substitutes for content. Our films are far more subtle. Kurasawa's movies for example, like *Throne of Blood*. The swordplay is beautiful, the strategy elegant, the end tragic."

"Now you're a film critic? Kurasawa stole the plot from Shakespeare."

"You don't like the classics? Come on, you can't beat the blind swordsman."

"You don't really believe someone could do that, do you?"

"It doesn't matter. It makes a great story."

They drove in silence for a few minutes.

"Maybe you're right," Genzo said. "About using a bomb."

"I thought you said the yakuza didn't use bombs."

"Boss will find a way to plant the story. Maybe make it look like the hotel wouldn't pay protection. Something like that."

"We could put it in a serving cart," Futoshi said, "like in the movie."

The two men argued about the merits of American and Japanese movies all the way back into town.

FIFTY-SIX

It was evening in Osaka. There had been a few aftershocks but nothing serious. Nick and Selena were getting ready to go down to the hotel dining room. Selena stood in front of the mirror, looking unhappy. She was wearing a loose gray shirt that covered the bandage on her arm and a black skirt. The arm hurt when she moved it.

"What's the matter?" Nick asked.

"I haven't got anything to wear. Nobuyasu ruined my best blouse."

"You look great, don't worry about it."

"That's easy for you to say."

"Because it's true. You look great."

He walked over, put his arms around her, and kissed her on the back of her neck.

"I booked us on a flight to Tokyo tomorrow morning. There's a plane leaving for California three hours after we get to Narita. We'll be home the next day."

"Good. I can't wait to get out of here."

"How's the arm?"

"Sore and stiff, but it will be fine. So far there's no sign of any infection."

"I wonder if they'll dig out that gold?"

"Wouldn't you?" Selena said. "There can't be anything left of the tunnel, but they might be able to find it using ground radar."

"It might be better if it stayed buried, along with those swords."

"I never thought I'd say this, but I think you're right, at least about the Muramasa.

When I pulled it from that suit of armor, it
felt like it came alive in my hands. It was the
same in the museum. When I was fighting, it
was as if it had a mind of its own.
Muramasa's swords were supposed to be
bloodthirsty, possessed. After that duel with
Nobuyasu, I can believe it."

"A demon sword?"

"It was really strange, Nick."

"You ready to go downstairs?"

"I guess."

The dining room was modern and
pleasantly lit. A long sushi bar ran along one
side. A buzz of conversation filled the room.
Most of the tables in the restaurant were
taken, but Nick had made a reservation. A
hostess seated them. Looking around, Nick
saw only a few Westerners.

"The food must be good here," he said.
"Most of the clientele are Japanese. It's a
good sign."

"I'm in the mood for Kobe beef," Selena
said.

"Sounds like a plan."

They ordered a bottle of wine to go with
the beef.

Selena sipped her wine. "I meant what I
said earlier."

"About working in the field?"

"Yes."

"It's been the better part of a year since
the Project was shut down. We've had
several jobs with Harker since then. None of
them turned out to be dangerous, like what
we used to do."

"Until now," Selena said.

"Sure. But this is the exception."

A waiter approached the table, wheeling a cart before him.

Nick's ear began burning. He tugged on it.

"Shit."

"What's wrong?" Selena asked.

"I don't know. I've got a bad feeling."

Unconsciously, he reached for the gun he usually had with him. It wasn't there. He looked at the waiter bringing the food. The man had his head down over the cart. Nick couldn't see his face. The man was dressed like the other waiters, but something was out of place. Then Nick saw his shoes. They were brown, scuffed. Everyone else had shoes of polished black.

Nick stood, his chair falling backward. The man looked at him. Nick saw something dark in his eyes.

Suddenly he pushed the cart hard toward Nick, turned and ran. The cart struck the table and tipped over. A cardboard box fell out onto the floor. A cell phone was taped to the top of the box. Wires came out of the box, connected to the phone.

"Bomb!" Nick yelled. "Bomb! Get out!"

People panicked and began screaming. Glassware and plates shattered as tables overturned. Nick looked at the bomb and knew he had seconds at the most. He reached down and ripped the phone away from the package, tearing the wires loose. As he did, it buzzed in his hand.

He stood there with the phone in his hand, surrounded by the chaos in the dining room. The man who had brought the cart was gone.

"Nick," Selena said.

"It's all right. It's not going to go off."

He was still standing there, the phone clutched in his hand, when the police poured into the room.

FIFTY-SEVEN

The police questioned Nick and Selena for an hour, and then let them go. They recognized Selena from the newspaper photographs taken at the museum. Witnesses had seen the phony waiter push the serving cart toward Nick and run away. If the bomb had gone off, it would have taken out half the room and killed dozens of people. The cell phone was meant to trigger the blast.

Nick was a hero, but he didn't feel like one.

They went back to their room.

"What a day," Selena said. "I don't believe this."

"We would've been turned into hamburger if that had gone off."

"And now we're stuck here. The police want to interview us again tomorrow."

"That bomb was meant for us," Nick said.

"You think it was the yakuza?"

Nick held a finger to his lips.

"It must be them. Kobayashi getting even."

He picked up a pad of hotel notepaper and wrote on it.

Not Kobayashi. Yamamoto. I think the room is bugged.

Selena read the note.

"You think he'll try again?" Selena said, playing along.

"Maybe, but we're probably okay for tonight. No way I can get to sleep. I need to stretch my legs. You want to come with me?"

They left the room, took the elevator down to the lobby, and walked outside. It was another warm night. The streets were crowded. There were always crowds in Japan, no matter where you went or what time of day it was.

They began walking. Sometimes they paused to look into a store window. Nick used the reflections to check for a tail. He saw no one suspicious.

"What makes you think it was Yamamoto?" Selena asked.

"Kobayashi is old-school," Nick said. "A bomb in a crowded restaurant doesn't fit with his concept of honor. He wouldn't have any hesitation about killing us, but blowing up a big hotel restaurant and creating a lot of collateral damage isn't his style."

"Why do you think the room was bugged?"

"It's the only explanation that makes sense. Kobayashi is out of the game. If the room is bugged, Yamamoto would have heard me talking on the phone with Harker."

"You can't be certain it was him."

"Let's find a place to sit down. I'll call Harker. She'll think of something."

"If it was Yamamoto, we're in trouble," Selena said.

They walked until they came to a small park, found a bench, and sat. Nick took out his phone and called Elizabeth.

She picked up.

"When are you coming home, Nick?"

"There's been a problem, Director."

Nick told her what had happened and that he thought Yamamoto was behind it.

"You're certain it wasn't the yakuza?" Elizabeth asked.

"It doesn't fit. Kobayashi is the only one with real motivation to want us dead, but it's not his style. The rest of the yakuza don't care. Hell, they're probably thanking us for giving them a chance to take over."

"You realize what this means? If it's Yamamoto, the only way to get him off your back is to expose him. That's exactly the kind of thing I didn't want to see happen."

"Hey, Director, I didn't call the shots here. That bomb would have killed dozens of innocent people, along with us. It doesn't say a lot for letting Yamamoto get away with it."

"Damn it, Nick. All right, I have to talk with Clarence about this. In the meantime, stay out of sight."

She disconnected. Nick looked at the phone.

"I take it she's not happy?" Selena said.

"Nope. In fact, I'd say she's pissed."

"She'll get over it."

"Let's find a different hotel for the rest of the night. It's better if no one knows where we are."

"What about tomorrow?"

"I guess that depends on what Harker figures out."

FIFTY-EIGHT

The next morning Nick and Selena were getting ready to go to the police station for their interview when Elizabeth called.

"The restaurant had cameras," she said. "There are excellent shots of the bomber. Facial recognition software turned up a hit."

"Who is he?"

"His name is Futosi Takahashi. He's an agent at the PSIA. He works directly under Yamamoto."

"If the guy knew what he was doing, he'd never have been caught on cameras like that."

"I'm getting all of this through DCI Hood. He's angry. He considered Yamamoto to be almost a friend. When I told him what I'd discovered about Yamamoto and Nobuyasu, I thought he was going to have a stroke. Clarence has strong ideas of right and wrong, a personal code of honor. Maybe it has something to do with his southern heritage, I don't know. What Yamamoto has done feels like a personal betrayal. It gives everyone who works in the intelligence agencies a bad name."

"That wouldn't be hard to do," Nick said.

"Nick…"

"Okay, sorry. What's he going to do?"

"He told me he'd handle it."

"What does that mean? Is Yamamoto going down, or not?"

"We have to trust Hood. But I can guess at what he might be planning."

"Which is?"

"If he's confronted, Yamamoto will deny any knowledge of what this man Takahashi was doing. I wouldn't be surprised if Takahashi had already disappeared, permanently. There's no way to prove Yamamoto ordered him to kill you. But there are other ways to make sure he doesn't walk away from this."

"Go on."

"As I see it, there are two possibilities. One would be to publicly expose Nobuyasu's ties with the yakuza drug business and how Yamamoto protected him. The proof is in the files I have. Langley might be able to find out what Nobuyasu was using to blackmail him. If any of that got out, Yamamoto would be finished."

"I wouldn't lose any sleep over that," Nick said. "You said there were a two possibilities. What's the other one?"

"A public exposé would threaten the stability of the current government. It could lead to new elections and the possibility of a right wing takeover. I don't think that's going to happen. I think Hood will find a way that avoids any public perception of corruption or illegal behavior."

"We certainly wouldn't want that, would we?"

"You of all people know that governments are always hiding things."

"That doesn't mean it's right. Particularly in this case."

"Which do you think is better? Yamamoto goes down in flames with big headlines, or something happens that removes the problem without creating waves?"

"As long as he gets what's coming to him, I don't care," Nick said.

"I think I can guarantee it won't be long before that happens," Elizabeth said.

FIFTY-NINE

Daichi Yamamoto sat in his study, a glass of whiskey in his hand. Heavy drapes were drawn across the windows, darkening the room. He'd shut off the phones.

Outside the quiet confines of his home, life went on as always in Tokyo. Yamamoto had always loved Tokyo. He was too young to remember the incendiary bombs of World War II and the fires that had swept through the city, killing a hundred thousand people. By the time he'd been born, Japan had become one of the great economic powers of the world and Tokyo had risen from the ashes like the mythical Phoenix, a giant metropolis of concrete and steel.

Soft music played in the background. Yamamoto had acquired a taste for Western classical music, especially Mozart and Bach. Usually the complex musical arrangements and changing moods of the two great composers soothed him and helped him think through whatever was on his mind.

Usually, but not today. Today his mind was overwhelmed with shame.

His personal weaknesses had allowed him to become ensnared in Nobuyasu's web of greed and deceit, and now those weaknesses were about to be exposed.

He emptied his glass and poured another.

Earlier, he'd gotten a call from the American CIA director, Hood. He'd been afraid it would come to this. When Takahashi had failed to kill the Americans in the hotel, he knew he had lost control. It was all going to come out, his corruption, his secrets.

Everything.

A memory came to him of a spring many years ago, when he was a boy. His father had taken him to Osaka Castle to view the cherry blossoms. Yamamoto had been about five years old. He remembered bright sunlight, the delicate blossoms drifting through the air, the towering castle rising into clear, blue sky. His father had gestured at the trees, then at the ground where fallen blossoms were strewn about.

"You see the blossoms? How fragile and beautiful they are?"

"Yes, father. But they are all falling. It is sad."

His father had nodded, pleased that his young son had come to the heart of things.

"That is one of the reasons we appreciate them. They remind us that the seasons of life come and go. They teach us that beauty is fleeting. That nothing stays the same. Nothing is permanent."

Yamamoto smiled at the memory. A pistol lay on the end table next to the chair where he sat. In the old days, a man as powerful as he would have gathered a few witnesses. He would have arranged his robes carefully, sitting on a white sheet of finest silk. He would have formally atoned for his misconduct through the ritual of seppuku. He would have written a poem, perhaps, for the occasion. Then when he had opened his belly and was about to succumb to the pain, his second would have struck his head from his shoulders.

He would have been remembered, respected, his honor regained through his act of atonement, in keeping with the samurai traditions of his culture. But now there were no more samurai. Now there was no way to regain his honor. Today's society had no respect for such actions of personal redemption.

Yamamoto picked up the pistol and held it to his temple. He thought of the cherry blossoms falling and pulled the trigger.

SIXTY

Everyone had gathered in Elizabeth's office. Ronnie and Lamont sat on the couch across from Nick and Selena. Stephanie was at her console. Elizabeth was behind her desk. There was something comforting about the familiar grouping.

Burps strolled in and jumped onto the couch. He climbed onto Selena's lap and began purring and kneading her leg. He looked up at her with a pleased expression on his face, drooling.

"Good thing I'm wearing my old jeans today," she said.

"The place looks a little worse for wear," Nick said. "What happened to George Washington?"

"I haven't had a chance to get everything repaired yet," Elizabeth said. "Washington suffered a lot of damage. I took the painting to the Smithsonian. They'll restore it."

"Sounds like you had a hell of a time in Japan," Lamont said. "Did you get to see any geishas?"

Nick shook his head. "Nope. No geishas."

"Did you hear about Yamamoto?" Elizabeth asked.

"No. What about him?"

"He killed himself yesterday. The official explanation is that he had an incurable cancer and had decided to take the quick way out."

"I can't say I'm sorry to hear it. Did he really kill himself, or did we help him out?"

"If you mean did we pull the trigger? No, we didn't. He did that himself. It was a very Japanese thing to do."

"What happened?" Selena asked.

"DCI Hood had a little chat with him and explained what we'd learned about his relationship with Nobuyasu. He told Yamamoto he was holding off releasing the information as a courtesy, out of consideration for the times he had helped the United States in the past. He suggested that Yamamoto might want to take some time to prepare for what was coming."

"That's sneaky," Lamont said. "Freak the guy out so he kills himself."

"What did you expect?" Ronnie said. "Hood runs the CIA. Those guys define sneaky."

"Yamamoto deserved it," Nick said.

"That's hard, man," Lamont said.

"What's going to happen with the gold?" Selena said.

"It's going to remain a mystery," Elizabeth said. "As far as most people are concerned, it's a myth. It can stay buried, along with Nobuyasu."

"He got what he wanted, in the end," Nick said. "The sword and the gold."

"Didn't do him a lot of good, did it?" Ronnie said.

"I wish we could have saved those swords," Selena said.

"Not me," Nick said. "The only sword I want to see from now on is the kind you stick through the olives in martinis."

Selena looked at Nick. He was smiling, happy.

He's in his element. He wouldn't know what to do if all of this went away. He's never going to quit.

The thought made her sad.

"We have a new client," Elizabeth said.

Notes

The history of Japan's feudal period is filled with events that make today's action movies look tame. A lot of blood was spilled across the islands before stability under the shoguns was established. The Emperor, sacred and secluded, was at the mercy of powerful generals who controlled armies composed of thousands of samurai. Highly trained, highly disciplined, skilled with a variety of lethal weapons, armed with the two swords, the samurai were known for their fanatical loyalty and heroism. They deserve the reputation that has been assigned to them. They were ruthless in battle. It was a ruthless age.

The films of Akira Kurosawa are a window into the world of feudal Japan. *The Seven Samurai* has been remade several times, but never in a way that captures the raw courage and heroism of the original film. *Throne of Blood,* mentioned in the book, is an adaptation of Shakespeare's Macbeth as it would have played out in the time of the shoguns. These are two great movies.

You may have seen *Shogun*, the made for TV adaptation of James Clavell's sweeping novel set at the beginning of the Tokugawa shogunate. It's well done and captures many of the nuances of that period in Japanese history. It's well worth seeing.

The Sword is based on a real sword known as the Honjo Masamune. It was handed over to the police at the end of the war by Iyeasu Tokugawa, a descendent of the Shogun by the same name who united Japan. Obedience to the emperor's command to surrender meant cooperating with the occupying forces. With a typical sense of Japanese honor and propriety, Tokugawa wanted to set an example for the other aristocratic leaders of defeated Japan.

An American sergeant picked up the sword, his name recorded as "Coldy Bilmor" in the police log. It has never been seen since. Most of the swords collected were melted down. Others came back to the United States as souvenirs. No one knows if the Honjo Masamune still exists or where it might be.

Masamune lived in the late thirteenth and early fourteenth centuries. He is the greatest maker of swords in Japan's history, and that tells you a lot. There were many great sword smiths who created weapons of enduring beauty and craftsmanship, but none whose swords were as valued as Masamune's. That such weapons could have been created with the technology of the time is extraordinary.

Muramasa lived at a later date. Many of his swords have survived and are displayed in museums. Legend holds that his swords are cursed and must drink blood before being placed back in their scabbards. This demonic aspect of his blades is popular in contemporary Japanese entertainment and games.

Toyotomi Hideyoshi was a real person. He rose from obscurity and a common birth to become the most powerful daimyo in Japan. A great general and skilled strategist, he built the castle at Osaka.

The story of the treasure known as the *Tenshou Ooban* is well known in Japan. What you read in the book is an accurate description of the legend of the treasure. Whether or not Hideyoshi took the money destined for the Korean armies and buried it, I can't say. But it's a heck of a story.

The Shinto shrine in Osaka that I describe does not exist, although Toyotomi Hideyoshi built many shrines in the area. I have tried to describe a typical shrine built in the older style. The sacred spirit of the shrine is called a *kami* in Japanese. It can be represented as a mirror.

I've been to Japan. It's a place filled with beauty and darkness, with an ancient and complex culture Westerners will never fully understand. If you have an opportunity to go there, go ahead, you won't regret it.

Thanks for reading my book. I hope you have enjoyed it.

Alex Lukeman
June, 2019

Acknowledgements

It's impossible to give credit to all the anonymous people who fill the Internet with information. I often search for historical details, climate and geography notes, and pictures of places I have not personally experienced. Hats off to all of you.

Neil Jackson keeps creating great covers. He always comes up with something interesting.

My wife Gayle, for more reasons than I can list.

You, the reader. You are why I do this. Thank you.

*****

If you liked this book, please consider leaving a positive review. You can find a box with a link for leaving a review on the page for the book. Reviews are essential for a writer's success, and I am no exception.

Be the first to know when I have a new book coming out by subscribing to my infrequent newsletter. No spam, ads, or busy emails, only a brief announcement now and then. Just click on the link below. You can unsubscribe at any time...

http://bit.ly/2kTBn85

About the Author

Alex Lukeman writes action/adventure thrillers featuring the Project, a covert intelligence unit operating under the radar. He is the author of the award-winning books *The Tesla Secret* and *High Alert*. He likes riding old, fast motorcycles and playing guitar, usually not at the same time. You can email him at alex@alexlukeman.com. He loves hearing from readers and promises he will get back to you.

Made in the USA
Middletown, DE
23 February 2021

34285144R00177